MAX

BEST FRIEND. HERO. MARINE.

WRITTEN BY JENNIFER LI SHOTZ

BASED ON A SCREENPLAY WRITTEN BY
BOAZ YAKIN & SHELDON LETTICH

HARPER

An Imprint of Harper Collins*Publishers*

Max

 For information address HarperCollins Children's Books, a division of HarperCollins Publishers, 195 Broadway, New York, NY 10007.
www.harpercollinschildrens.com

alloyentertainment

Produced by Alloy Entertainment
1700 Broadway
New York, NY 10019
www.alloyentertainment.com

ISBN 978-0-06-242039-8 (pbk.)

Typography by Natalie C. Sousa

16 17 18 19 CG/OPM 20 19 18 17 16 15 14
❖
First Edition

ONE

THE LATE-AFTERNOON SUN POURED IN THROUGH Justin's bedroom window. A glare reflected off his computer screen, but he couldn't get up to pull down the blinds: He was right in the middle of a seriously epic battle against an entire military unit. And at the moment, he was winning.

It was another hot summer day in Lufkin, Texas—which meant that it was another day Justin had spent almost entirely in his room.

His best friend, Chuy, who was practically his only friend, sat on Justin's bed and watched him play the video game. Chuy let out a couple of whoops and "Dudes!" as Justin took down soldier after soldier.

As Justin finished the level, his computer's disc drive whirred and clicked. He was also burning a copy of the game for Chuy to give to his older cousin, Emilio. Emilio paid Justin cash for clean copies of the latest games, as long as they had no security codes or encryption. It wasn't like Justin was a computer genius or anything; he'd just figured out how to do it . . . and how to sell them. Which, it turned out, was a pretty decent way for a fourteen-year-old to make some extra money. And he didn't have to leave his room to do it.

Chuy bounced on Justin's bed, impatiently waiting for the disc.

"Seriously, man, what's taking so long?" Chuy asked from his perch on the edge of Justin's bed.

"Just a couple more minutes. Chill." Justin clicked away at the controller as a steady stream of soldiers fired away on-screen. The virtual army let out a series of grunts and pumped their fists in the air or fell to the ground.

Justin used to play this video game with his older brother, Kyle. More accurately, Justin used to lose to Kyle on a regular basis. But now Kyle was a real soldier, fighting in Afghanistan, on the other side of the world. Sometimes Justin tried to picture Kyle as one of these guys, but it was just too weird. He couldn't imagine his brother shooting anyone.

Chuy got up and began pacing the room. He ran a hand through his short, curly hair and pulled up his sagging shorts.

"Dude, I can't focus with you acting like a caged animal back there. Cut it out," Justin said. Chuy always had more energy than he knew what to do with. His best friend sat back down on the edge of the bed, bouncing his knee up and down. Finally, the disc drive stopped spinning.

"Here you go," Justin said, hitting Eject and picking up the burned disc from the computer tray. "Clean master. No codes, no encryption. You can't rush perfection, Chuy."

Chuy rolled his eyes and reached for the disc in Justin's outstretched hand.

"Yeah, yeah, I get it. You're like the ninja master," Chuy said.

"You got that right." Justin gripped the disc tightly so that Chuy couldn't take it from him. "Tell Emilio I want an extra two hundred for this one."

Chuy's eyes widened as he said, "Uh, what was that? 'Cause I know I didn't hear you right."

"He's selling the *Assassin's Creed* I ripped all the way up in Austin. I think he can afford a couple hundred bucks." Justin released the disc into Chuy's hand.

"You don't want any beef with my cousin, man. Trust me," Chuy replied.

Justin shrugged. "Two hundred more, or this is the last one." He spun around in his desk chair to face his computer again. He waited for Chuy's comeback, but, surprisingly, none came.

From behind him, Justin heard the bedsprings squeak as his friend quickly stood up.

"Hello, Mr. Wincott," Chuy said in a stiff voice.

With a start, Justin turned around to face his dad, Ray, who filled the doorframe. Even in his Open Range Storage jumpsuit, his dad still managed to look like a Marine. His posture was ramrod straight, his hair buzzed military short, his expression stern.

"Hello, Chuy," said Justin's dad.

Chuy shifted nervously from foot to foot. "Uh, I was just leaving. Bye, Justin. See you around." Chuy shuffled toward the door. Justin's dad stepped aside, and Chuy slipped his skinny body by him like a guilty cat sneaking past a dog.

"Son." His father nodded.

"Hey, Dad." Justin started to turn back toward his computer.

"I need you to help me unload some stuff from the truck."

"I'll be there in a minute," Justin replied.

"Now," his dad said sternly.

Justin sighed and pushed back his chair. His dad was always bossing him around. Maybe his brother, Kyle, was okay with doing whatever their dad asked, but Justin didn't need obedience training.

"Fine," Justin said, and followed his dad out of the room. On his way out, he noticed that Chuy had left the disc behind on his bed. He smiled to himself. Leave it to Chuy to be so freaked out by Justin's dad that he forgot what he had come here for. Emilio was pretty hard-core—possibly even in a gang—and he wasn't going to be happy when he learned that Chuy had misplaced his new game.

His dad limped through the hallway and down the stairs, Justin following close behind. It never ceased to amaze him how fast his dad could move, especially with the leg injury that had gotten him sent home from the first Gulf War. Justin and Kyle weren't even alive when that had happened, and they'd never known their dad without his limp. It was just something they'd grown up with, and wasn't a big deal. But sometimes Justin felt as if the injury had only made Kyle worship their dad even more.

Kyle had followed in their father's footsteps in a million ways. He worked hard, he did well in school, and now he was a Marine and a hero, just like their dad. Not Justin, though. It wasn't exactly on purpose, but he couldn't have been more opposite from either one of them.

Although there was one thing Kyle had done differently from their dad. Justin's brother wasn't just a regular Marine—he was specially trained to work with a military working dog, who was stationed with him in Afghanistan. Not only did their parents think Kyle was the perfect son, but they talked about his dog, Max, as though he was their third child. Justin felt like he'd been one-upped by a canine.

Justin followed his dad out of the house and into the backyard. The hot Texas air immediately enveloped them. What also surrounded Justin was his dad's temper.

"I was expecting to see you at work this morning," his dad said without looking at Justin, surveying the yard.

"So you could pay me eight bucks an hour sweeping your floors?" Justin shook his head. "No thanks."

His dad stopped by the sliding patio doors that led into the living room. Justin's mom, Pamela, was inside vacuuming. She had just gotten home from her job at Walmart and still had her name tag pinned to her shirt. Justin watched her through the glass doors as he braced himself for his dad's response.

"I guess you'd rather I pay you to sit on your butt playing video games all day," his dad said.

Justin clenched and unclenched his fists. He knew exactly where this conversation was going. "Better than running some stupid storage place where people keep the junk they should just throw away."

His dad's whole body tensed. Justin took a step backward. Maybe he had pushed his dad too far, but he wasn't the perfect son—that role was already filled—and he wasn't about to be.

"That junk puts food in your smart mouth, son." His dad's eyes were lit up with anger. "And I don't run it. I *own* it. Most folks are lucky for the chance to punch a time card, but not me. I'm my own boss."

"Maybe you are. Maybe you were even Kyle's boss. But you're not mine," Justin said.

Justin could see his dad's jaw tightening and the muscles in his face twitching.

"I advise you to leave your brother out of this," his dad said coldly. "At least he knows what it means to put in a hard day's work. And to show some respect."

Justin rolled his eyes. "Yeah, and that 'hard work' is doing us a lot of good halfway around the world. He's not even here to help out."

"Stop now, Justin." His dad took a step toward him, his eyes locked on his son's.

Justin had definitely gone too far this time. He turned away and headed for the driveway, looking for where he'd left his bike. He could ride to Chuy's house and spend the night there. Justin stepped onto the concrete and heard his dad's footsteps following close behind. Justin spun around so they were face-to-face.

"What, Dad? Is this the part where you tell me again how Kyle is so perfect because he's a Marine just like you?" Justin asked.

His dad's eyes practically bulged out of his head. "Justin, I swear—"

Before his dad could finish the sentence, they both heard the sound of a car door slamming out front.

They looked around the house and saw a black four-door sedan in their driveway. Two men in military uniforms headed for the walkway leading to their front door.

"Dad—" Justin started to say, but his dad held up a hand to silence him, his body suddenly coiled like a spring. They watched the two men walk up the path and out of sight as they neared the front door. There was something in his dad's face that Justin had never seen there before: fear. His mouth was clamped tightly shut, and his forehead was wrinkled with worry. Soldiers at their door could only mean one thing . . . Kyle. What had happened to him? Had he been hurt? Justin felt queasy.

"Stay here, Justin," his dad said in a raspy voice.

His dad headed back across the yard. He stepped quickly through the sliding glass door and into the house just as the doorbell rang. He crossed the living room in a few purposeful strides while Justin's mom opened the front door. Justin watched from the back-yard as if it were a silent movie: His mom stepped back when she saw the men in uniform. His father caught her before she collapsed in shock. His father lowered his head, his body shaking. Then, finally, a single sound pierced the quiet—his mother's choked sob.

That's when Justin knew for sure: His brother was dead. Kyle was dead.

TWO

"NICE ONE, J-BIRD." KYLE WAS TEACHING JUSTIN HOW *to hit baseballs into a net in their backyard. Kyle patted his kid brother on the head.*

"Gotta work on your follow-through," Kyle said as he took the bat from Justin's eight-year-old hands. "Now are you ready for some lemonade?"

Justin nodded and smiled to himself as he followed his big brother into the house.

Justin ripped open the plastic packaging of his new clothing. He pulled out a formal white shirt and held it up, shaking out the sleeves. The fabric was stiff, and the collar was even stiffer. He tugged at the strip of cardboard tucked inside the collar and tossed it down on his floor. He unbuttoned the shirt and slipped it on over his white T-shirt, then started the work of buttoning it back up. He tucked it into the black suit pants and buckled the thick leather belt. The cloth hung heavily against his legs, and the belt weighed a thousand pounds. He didn't even have the jacket on yet, and he was already hot. He wondered how some men could wear these stuffy clothes every single day.

Justin had never had a reason to wear a suit before, and he'd never thought that his brother's funeral would be the first time. He could hear his mom crying softly on the other side of the wall and his father's low voice comforting her.

The morning sun peeked through the windows. It was another bright, blue-skied day, but Justin just felt dark inside. He hadn't known it was possible to feel this lousy. Sad wasn't quite the right word; it was more like . . . hopeless? Alone?

With a sigh, he sat down on the edge of his unmade bed. He jammed his feet into the cruel-looking black dress shoes. The clock on his dresser told him he had twenty minutes to kill before his family left for the church. He didn't want to walk around in these miserable clothes for a moment longer than necessary, so he lay back on his mound of pillows and looked up at his posters of indie bands and obscure old movies. Kyle had helped him hang some of them up before he'd left for the Marines. Kyle's room, of course, was decorated with sports posters and trophies. He used to tease Justin about his "emo indie" taste.

Justin closed his eyes so he couldn't see the pictures hanging all over his walls. Everything reminded him of Kyle now.

"Kyle! Kyyyyyyyyle!"

Kyle came running through the living room in a T-shirt and boxer shorts, his face screwed up with worry.

"Justin—what is it? Are you okay?"

"I need help."

Kyle ran a hand through his hair. "Justin, what's up? I'm studying for a trigonometry test, man. What does a fourth grader need?"

"Help. I need help." Justin pointed at the television, a black plastic controller wedged into his grubby hand. "I'm stuck on level four, and I really need the gold sword, or I can't get to level five. Can you please help me?"

For a second, he thought Kyle was going to be mad at him, but his brother just burst out into one of his huge grins—the kind that made their mother giggle and forgive him for anything.

"J-Bird, you want me to fail my test?"

"No," Justin laughed. "But I really want you to help me get this sword."

Kyle sighed and dropped down onto the floor next to Justin. They leaned back against the couch together, and Kyle took the remote.

"Watch the master at work, kiddo. And don't forget how good you have it in elementary school."

Justin watched in awe as Kyle easily made his way through the caves and flames and monster hordes on-screen.

"Dude, you rock at this game. Now I want you to fail your test so you can always help me," Justin said.

The doorbell rang downstairs. Justin didn't move. It rang again, echoing through the quiet house. He waited for the sound of his parents' footsteps, but the house was silent except for his mom's hushed weeping. The bell rang a third time, and Justin finally gathered the energy to push himself up off his bed. He felt groggy, like he was half asleep. He trudged through the house to the front door and swung it open. A blast of summer heat came at him. A limo driver in a dark suit stood sweating on the porch, his long, dark car parked across the driveway behind him. He barely looked old enough to have a driver's license.

"Hi, I'm here to pick up the"—the driver checked a folded piece of paper in his hand—"the Wincotts. To go to the, uh . . ." He trailed off.

"Yeah, that's us," Justin said. "We'll be right out."

Justin shut the door and went back upstairs to his parents' room. He listened for a moment, then knocked lightly.

"Yes?" came his father's gravelly voice.

"The driver's here."

"Okay, Justin, thanks. We'll be right out," his dad said.

"Are you ready, honey?" his mom asked softly.

"Yeah, Mom. I'm ready. I just need to get my jacket."

"Don't tell Mom and Dad," Justin begged.

"What's it worth to you, kiddo?" Kyle started his car as Justin buckled his seat belt. They pulled away from the middle school and headed toward home.

"No, seriously, Kyle—don't tell them!"

"I won't, Justin." Kyle turned to look at him. "Just be glad I'm the one who answered the phone and was able to come get you." His expression turned serious. "What happened in there?"

Justin looked down at his knees, then out the window. He didn't know how to tell Kyle that he'd gotten in a fight over a stupid bike. Or that he'd been sucker-punched. Or that he'd managed not to hit back, because he didn't think it was worth it.

Despite all that, Justin had still gotten in trouble.

Kyle had never gotten into trouble in his life—and no one had ever been mad at him. Kyle probably never felt so angry at other people that he couldn't look at them sometimes, like Justin did. Kyle had never felt like the weird kid in a room full of jocks. He'd never been picked on. Kyle wouldn't understand.

"I don't know. It's just . . . I didn't like the way he was talking about my friend's bike. So I called him on it." Justin squirmed in his seat. Kyle kept his hands on the steering wheel and his gaze straight ahead. "But I didn't punch him, I swear."

They stopped at a red light, and Kyle turned to look at his little brother again. "I'm proud of you, J-Bird."

Justin thought he'd misheard him. "You're what?"

"I'm proud of you, man. Good for you for standing up for a friend. And for not hitting back."

"Thanks," Justin mumbled. He fought the urge to smile at his brother's words. He felt a rush of happiness, like

he'd just won a championship game or something. Justin shifted in his seat and felt something bumping against his ankle. He leaned down and picked up a folder stuffed with forms and papers. On the front was a drawing of a bird with a flag in its mouth, resting atop the Earth. It was the U.S. Marine Corps logo.

"What's this?" Justin asked, happy to change the subject.

Kyle cracked a huge grin and said, "That, my friend, is my future."

It took Justin a second to absorb what he was hearing. "Wait—are you saying—did you—"

"Yeah, kiddo. I'm in. I enlisted."

"You enlisted? You're going to be a Marine? Just like that?" Justin wasn't surprised that Kyle wanted to do it—he'd known all his life that his brother planned to follow in their dad's footsteps. He just hadn't realized it was happening so soon. Justin's heart sank, and whatever happy feeling he'd just had was replaced by a sharp pang in his chest. Kyle was leaving?

Kyle reached over and tousled Justin's hair. "Just like that, man. Just like that. Don't worry, you'll get used to missing me."

Justin punched him on the shoulder. "I won't miss you at all, dude."

He tried to look at his big brother, but his throat felt tight, and he had to look away.

Justin held open the front door for his parents. His father held his mom tightly around her waist—almost as though he was keeping her upright—as they walked toward the waiting limousine. The driver stood by the open door, his hands clasped in front of him and his eyes cast downward. He looked miserable, as if he thought he was going to catch something from Justin and his family.

Justin's mom's wavy black hair was pushed back from her face. Her eyes were red and swollen, and she clutched a packet of tissues. His dad's face was a frozen mask. He looked so out of place in his new suit, especially with his sunburned neck peeking out above the collar. His jaw was set, his mouth pinched closed, his eyes glassy and unreadable. Like a soldier. He'd gotten up early to buzz his hair into a precise Marine cut.

The three of them slid into the back of the air-conditioned car. The driver shut the door, and the silence closed in around them. Justin's mom looked at him as if she were just realizing he was there.

"You look very handsome, honey," she said. "In your suit."

"Thanks, Mom."

No one spoke for the rest of the ten-minute drive to the church. The fabric of the white shirt rubbed against Justin's neck. He swatted at it, but it just kept scratching him. His feet felt cramped in the stiff shoes. It was going to be a rough day, that much was clear. It made him wonder how Kyle had ever gotten used to wearing his uniform all the time—but Kyle wasn't a complainer. Plus, Justin knew that his brother loved his "suit of armor," as he called his full combat gear. Even his military dog, Max, wore an armored vest. That uniform had made everyone so proud of Kyle . . . Now he was going to be buried in it.

"Hello, handsome," his mom said to the laptop screen. She leaned in to the computer, as if it would actually bring her closer to her son.

"Hey, Ma." Kyle sat in a tent, wearing his fatigues. He looked tired.

"You getting enough rest, hon?" she asked.

"Mom, I'm in the Marines. That's not exactly our first priority." Kyle laughed.

"Well, I'm in the Momarines, and it's always my first priority," she shot back with a smile. "Tell your captain I said so."

"I'll get right on that."

Justin stomped through the kitchen, past his mom sitting at the round kitchen table with her laptop. He opened the fridge and rummaged around.

"Justin, say hi to your brother," his mom called out.

"Hi to your brother," Justin mumbled into the deli drawer.

"So he can hear you," she said. She swung the computer around toward Justin. Kyle's face filled the video-chat screen.

Justin waved, a big pretend smile plastered on his face. Then he stuck his face back into the fridge, looking for a snack.

She rolled her eyes at Kyle, who shook his head and grinned. "It's okay, Mom. He's just being fourteen."

A loud barking made them all jump.

"You want to say hi, too, Max?" Kyle asked. "Come here, boy."

Suddenly, a furry black snout and a loud snuffling sound filled the screen. Kyle and their mom burst out laughing. Justin turned around to see what was happening and couldn't help but crack a smile. Even Justin couldn't deny that the dog was pretty cute. Even though Justin had only met Max through video chat, he could tell that Max could be a goofball when he wasn't off saving lives. Maybe Kyle and his dog were more alike than Justin had first thought.

Justin's dad limped into the kitchen carrying a large toolbox. He waved at the wet nose and whiskers on-screen.

"Hey, son. Looks like you're letting your beard grow in, huh?"

"Very funny, Dad," Kyle said from somewhere behind the dog. "Max, tell Dad he's hilarious, would you?"

Max barked.

"Max, I heard you dug up a pretty good cache of weapons there, huh?" their dad said, leaning into the camera. "And you let Kyle lend a hand?"

Kyle scratched Max behind the ears. They pressed their heads together so they could both see the screen. "He did all the work," Kyle said. "Ain't that right, boy?"

"Can he really see us right now?" their mom asked.

"We're just a sea of pixels to a dog's eyes, Pamela," their dad said. "Don't mess with your mother like that, Kyle."

"Sir, yes, sir." Kyle saluted his dad.

"Max, teach that Marine how to give a proper salute, would you, boy?" their dad teased.

Kyle lifted up one of Max's front paws and held it up to the dog's brow.

"Well," their mom interrupted the banter, "I think you and Max deserve some kind of medal. You're both very brave."

"Oh, Ma, we're just doing our jobs."

"Yeah," Justin said, closing the fridge a little too firmly. "Kyle's so awesome even his frickin' dog is a hero."

The room went still.

"Justin," his dad snapped. "Show some respect."

"And while you're at it," his mom added, "don't you cuss in this house."

Justin slapped a slice of bread down on a plate. "I didn't cuss."

"Close enough," his mom said.

"Do I hear Justin swearing?" A new voice cut through the tension. Kyle looked up and slid to the side as a different face appeared on the screen. Justin recognized the familiar smirk and dirty-blond hair. It was Tyler Harne, his brother's best friend since forever. They had enlisted together, trained together, and now were stationed together. Another example of Kyle's blessed life. How many guys got shipped out across the globe and still got to be with their oldest buddy?

"Tyler!" his mom said. "Nice to see you."

"Hi, Mrs. W. Nice to see you, too. I got your boy covered here. Don't you worry about a thing."

"Thank you."

"Is that your pot roast I smell? That right there is the pride of Lufkin," Tyler said.

"Oh, I'm sure you're getting delicious pot roast in Afghanistan, Tyler," Justin's dad called out.

"If you call dehydrated meat delicious, sir, then yes, we are," Tyler replied.

"Are you boys staying out of trouble?" Justin's mom asked.

"We're making trouble, Mrs. W.," Tyler said. "For the bad guys, that is."

"Hooooorah!" Justin sneered. He had never been much of a Tyler fan. Tyler had pretty much spent Justin's entire childhood being extra nice to him in front of Justin's parents, and nasty to him when adults weren't around.

"Can it, Justin," his dad said in an icy tone.

Kyle and Tyler looked up as a deep voice said something unintelligible offscreen. They both stood up quickly.

"We got to go, guys," Kyle said. "Love you, Mom."

"Love you, hon." She kissed her fingertips, then placed them gently against the screen. "Justin, say good-bye to your brother."

Justin ignored her.

"Justin!" she snapped.

Justin barely had time to look up and see his brother's face before the computer went black.

III ★★★ THREE

HIS MOTHER'S SOBS CARRIED UP AND OVER THE SINGing of the church choir. Justin could feel the whole pew shake as she cried. Her sadness was overwhelming, but Justin didn't feel sad. He didn't feel much of anything.

Behind Justin and his parents, the pews were packed with friends and family that had known Kyle his entire life. Even his teachers and ex-girlfriends had come to pay their respects. Justin knew Kyle would find it hilarious to see all these people in one place—if it wasn't because it was his funeral, of course.

Justin tried to look anywhere but straight ahead at his brother's coffin. He gazed up at the arched ceiling for a minute, then down at the floor. He looked out the tall windows and counted the colors in the stained glass. He looked at the pastor's expression of concern. He wondered how long it had taken the man to perfect his funeral face. Justin watched the mouths of the singers, forming perfect *O*s. But his eyes were always led back to the casket in front of him.

The casket was dark wood, with gleaming handles and an American flag draped over the top. Next to it was a large photograph of a smiling Kyle posing in his uniform. Justin hated seeing the happy look on his brother's face—it only reminded him that he would never hear Kyle's laugh or see his big grin ever again.

Justin had barely said good-bye to Kyle when he was getting ready to ship out. They had played some hoops in the driveway that morning. Kyle's bags were packed, and his friends were going to drive him to the airport that afternoon. Kyle had told his parents they weren't allowed to take him—they all knew it would upset their mom too much.

Justin shifted in his seat. The wooden bench was uncomfortable—as were his shirt, shoes, and jacket. Every part of him felt unsettled and weird, inside and out. It was almost like he couldn't escape the ill-fitting clothes or the queasy feeling in his gut—or the ache that had settled in his chest since the day the two Marines had shown up at his front door.

If Justin was being honest with himself, he had been angry at Kyle the day he had shipped out. He didn't understand why his older brother had to leave their family—had to leave *him*. With Kyle gone, there would be no one else for their dad to focus on. Just Justin—who could never do anything right. Justin, who wanted to play video games all day. Justin, who didn't want to join the Marines.

And now that Kyle was never coming back, their dad would only start paying more attention to Justin, and their mom would only be more worried about him all the time.

The choir continued their hymn. The notes echoed up to the high ceiling, and Justin let the music fill his mind and clear away all his thoughts.

Suddenly, the wide double doors of the church flew open with a *bang*, interrupting the song. The old wooden seats creaked loudly as everyone in the room spun around to look at the late arrivals. Justin strained his neck to try and see the group of men silhouetted against the doorway. There were four of them, and they were all in military dress uniforms. One of the soldiers held a leash, at the end of which was a very familiar-looking black and tan dog. Though he'd never actually met the animal, Justin instantly recognized his long black snout and oversized, pointy black ears from the many video chats with his brother.

It was Max. He was bigger and slinkier than he appeared on camera, lean, but with muscles rippling under his fur. What was he doing here? Why wasn't he still in Afghanistan and teamed up with a new soldier?

Max stood in the doorway and sniffed the air. His head bobbed up and down as he strained against his collar. He took a few steps inside and sniffed at the ground. Justin thought he looked . . . nervous? Or maybe just confused? Suddenly, Max froze, his body tensed up, and his eyes grew round. Justin could tell he had found a familiar scent. Max bolted forward, but the man holding his leash tightened his grip and yanked back. He said a command to Max that Justin couldn't quite hear. Max just kept struggling against his leash, his two front paws coming off the ground.

One of the men in uniform walked up the aisle to Justin and his parents.

"I'm sorry we're late, Mr. and Mrs. Wincott," he

said, leaning over the pew. "We had a little tussle with Max here."

Justin couldn't believe it, but his mom actually smiled. There was a flash of happiness in her red-rimmed eyes. She looked at Max, then back up at the man.

"It's quite all right," she said.

"I'm Sergeant Reyes," the man went on. He had buzzed black hair and smiling eyes. "I trained your son and Max. After Kyle . . . after the incident, they sent Max back to us for an evaluation. He's been having a hard time since he got back. We thought, since we're located nearby . . . it might be a good thing for Max to be here today."

"You thought right," Justin's mom replied. "Kyle would have wanted it this way, I'm sure."

Across the room, Max whimpered and perked up his ears, as if he had heard Kyle's name. Sergeant Reyes nodded at the man holding Max's leash—or trying to hold Max's leash—mostly the man was getting dragged around by Max, who was using all of his well-trained brute strength to pull forward. Justin winced at the sight of the dog's desperate eyes and the sound of his whimpering. Max panted and strained to breathe as the soldier struggled to restrain him. But Max was stronger and more determined—the dog yanked so hard, Justin was actually worried for the man's arm. With a jolt, the leash flew out of his hand.

Max shot forward and crossed the room at lightning speed, stopping in front of Kyle's casket. He raised himself up on his hind legs and rested his front paws on top of the wood. He sniffed at the shiny handles, the flowers, and the flag.

Everyone in the church held their breath and watched. Finally, Max touched his nose to the flag atop Kyle's coffin and let out a mournful howl. Then—as if he'd confirmed something for himself—Max dropped onto the floor, spun in a circle, curled up into a ball, and lay down at the foot of the casket.

The crowd gasped, then loud sobs rang out across the room. Justin's mom gripped his dad's hand tightly and began to weep again. Justin saw his dad's lower lip begin to quiver. His dad nodded quickly at the pastor, who gestured to the choir. The first notes of a new hymn floated out over the crowd as Max howled along.

★ ★ ★

AS THE CEREMONY CAME TO AN END, JUSTIN DREADED the next step. They had to go to the cemetery to bury

Kyle. But first, Sergeant Reyes and his men had to get Max away from the coffin, which was basically impossible. Like Justin, Max didn't want to go.

Reyes used a hand signal and a verbal command, but Max ignored him. Then the handler pulled hard on Max's leash, and the dog went berserk. Everyone jumped as Max let out a series of harsh barks and howls. Justin didn't remember Max ever acting this crazy—Kyle always said he was the perfect dog. Max strained against his leash, snarling and thrashing his head around. He scratched at the floor.

It was terrible to watch. Justin had never seen an animal so upset before. In a way, though, Max was just doing what Justin wished he could do—scream and yell and let everyone know how pissed off he was at this whole stupid situation.

Sergeant Reyes turned to Justin's parents with a sheepish look on his face.

"I'm sorry," the sergeant said. "Max really was trained better than this."

"It's okay," Justin's mom said softly. "I understand how he feels."

The handler slowly managed to steer Max away from the casket, even as the dog continued to growl and bark. But just as they neared the front pew, where Justin and his parents stood watching, Max suddenly froze and locked his legs. He raised his black muzzle into the air and twitched his nose. He'd caught the scent of something, and it instantly calmed him down. Max sniffed at the air and took a step toward Justin's mom and dad. Sergeant Reyes instantly jumped in front of Max, shielding them from the unpredictable dog.

"It's okay," Justin's mom said. "I think he smells something—I think he recognizes us."

Reyes gave her a skeptical look, but moved slightly to the side, allowing Max to take another step forward. He sniffed at her legs, then at Justin's dad. Everyone in the church watched anxiously. Finally, Max nosed his way between the Wincotts and sat down right at Justin's feet. Nervously, Justin took a big step backward, putting a safe distance between him and Max. He could feel the eyes of everyone directed straight at him. Even the pastor watched from the altar.

"And who might you be, son?" Reyes asked.

"This is Kyle's brother," Justin's mom replied. "Justin."

Justin's dad looked ready to pounce on the dog if

it tried to hurt his wife or son. Max leaned forward and took a curious sniff at Justin. His long tail gave the slightest hint of a wag. Justin gulped and felt his hands get a bit sweaty. He'd never been a dog person like Kyle. The last time he'd been anywhere near a dog was with the twenty Chihuahuas that lived at Chuy's house, and those tiny furballs didn't count.

"Max seems to have figured out who you are," Reyes said to Justin, his voice warm and measured. The sergeant gave Justin a once-over, as if he were assessing a military situation. "Want to help us get him into the van?"

Justin shook his head. "No thanks."

Reyes held Justin's gaze for a long moment. Justin felt as if the man was trying to read his mind, so he looked away and down at the ground.

"It might go a lot easier if you did," Sergeant Reyes said, gesturing to the church doors—and the parking lot beyond them—with his thumb.

"Go on, Justin," his dad said, his voice hoarse. "Help the men out."

Justin shrugged. He hated that everyone was staring at him. Now he wasn't just Kyle's little brother, or even the dead Marine's little brother—he was the dead Marine's little brother who got sniffed by a crazy dog in church. Lufkin was too small of a town for that news to stay quiet for long.

"Okay, fine," he muttered.

Justin headed for the doors, Max trotting happily by his side. The handler gave Max some slack on his leash, and Max didn't pull away. Justin kept waiting for Max to turn psycho again, but he didn't.

The group stepped out into the sunlight and heat, and Max stuck next to Justin as they crossed the parking lot to the van. It was like Max was on a mission. Justin wondered if this is what Max did when he and Kyle were on patrol. Max was alert, and his big black-and-tan ears swerved from side to side, listening for danger. Justin almost wanted to laugh. What kind of danger did this dog expect to find in a tiny, boring Texas town?

Reyes opened the back doors, revealing a large metal box with one small window near the top. Max instantly lowered his front half to the ground and growled. All the fur on the back of his body stood on end. He barked at the crate as if it was his worst enemy. Sergeant Reyes sighed and grabbed a leather muzzle.

"All right," he said, facing his men. "Let's do this. Everybody ready?"

The soldiers nodded, although Justin thought they

looked anything but ready; instead it looked like they were dreading getting Max into the crate.

"On my count," Reyes said. "One. Two. Three—"

Three men circled Max from behind as Reyes approached from the front, the muzzle in his hand. Max backed up but couldn't get past the half circle of muscle behind him. His handler held the leash tightly. Reyes stepped forward and in one quick motion buckled the mesh leather cone over Max's nose. The dog yelped and swung his head from side to side. His whole body shook and his tail dropped between his legs.

Justin watched the scene with a heavy heart. Max hadn't done anything wrong, but he still had to be controlled. Once he was muzzled, Max began scratching fiercely at the ground and trying to knock the cone off his face with his front paws.

"Do you still need my help?" Justin asked. He didn't really want to put Max through any more pain.

"We still need to get him in the van," Reyes said. "Maybe you can just talk to him while we do it."

"Uh, okay. What should I say?"

"Anything you think he might want to hear," Reyes said.

Justin swallowed hard. Now that the dog wasn't able

to bite, the Marines closed in. Someone counted to three. Each man grabbed Max, and they lifted him up and into the crate. Max fought with all his might. He couldn't get out any real barks, but he growled loudly. He butted the men with his head, whipped them with his tail, and scratched at them with his giant paws. He landed a few good blows to a couple of their chests and to Reyes's cheek. The men grunted and struggled and eventually backed Max into the crate. Reyes closed the metal gate as quickly as possible.

It seemed so extreme to lock up a dog like that, but at the same time, Justin didn't know how else they would manage Max. He was one pissed-off dog, that was for sure.

Justin realized he hadn't said a word the entire time. Oops.

"Oh, sorry—I didn't talk to him."

Reyes brushed his messed-up hair back from his face and straightened his rumpled shirt. The other men rearranged their uniforms as well.

"It's okay," Reyes said. "That was actually Max on his best behavior. I think having you here calmed him down a bit."

"Seriously, that was calm?" Justin asked, astonished.

Reyes smiled and raised an eyebrow in acknowledgement. "Thanks, Justin." He held out his hand and Justin shook it. "Your brother talked about you a lot, you know."

Justin felt a dull throbbing in his chest. He hadn't known that. He always felt as though Kyle left and just stopped thinking about him—stopped being his brother, in fact. Hearing otherwise nearly knocked the breath out of him.

Reyes gave him a quick salute and climbed into the driver's seat of the van. Max's handler checked the lock on the crate and started to close the back doors.

"Wait!" Justin called out. He took a step forward. Max paced and spun in a slow circle inside his crate. His tail hung low between his back legs. He looked miserable. "Bye, Max," Justin said softly. Max looked up at him, and Justin was surprised to feel a surge of sadness. He had never met this dog before—why did he suddenly care what happened to him?

"Would you look at that," Justin's mom said. "He likes your voice, Justin."

Justin swallowed hard against the knot in his throat and told himself to get it together. He stood with his parents, and they all watched as Max dropped to the ground and put his head down on his front paws, as if all the fight was gone out of him—for the moment, anyway.

Max's handler closed the doors gently but firmly, and climbed into the passenger seat. The van pulled away, and Max was gone.

FOUR

PING.

Justin ignored the sound for the hundredth time.

Ping. Ping.

A stream of instant messages popped up on the left side of his computer screen. He didn't have to look at them to know they were all from Chuy. But Justin had other things to take care of—namely, a couple of dudes to take down so he could finish this level of his game.

He punched away at the controls, jamming at the knobs and pounding at the buttons as he made his way through the mayhem on his screen.

Ping. Ping. Ping. Ping.

Dude where r u? U got me worried. Write me back or else.

"Dude, leave me *alone*," Justin said out loud to the empty room. He slapped the controller down on his desk and hit the power button on his computer. The angry ninjas froze midkick and disappeared.

Justin stood up and paced around his room. All morning he'd been cooped up indoors. He hadn't even gone downstairs, except to grab some cereal for breakfast. On his way back to his room, he'd tried hard not to look at the closed door to his brother's bedroom. He hadn't set foot in there since Kyle died. And now, as he was trying to fill his summer vacation with video games, all he could think about was the empty room right down the hall. Would that space feel different now? Would he feel as if Kyle were still alive if he went into his room?

He also wondered what was inside the giant plastic footlocker that had arrived on their doorstep a couple of days ago. Every Marine got one of the lockers to hold their personal belongings, and Kyle's had been shipped back to them from Afghanistan. WINCOTT, KYLE, CORP. USMC was stenciled on it in bold paint. When it had arrived at their house, Justin's dad had dragged it upstairs and into Kyle's room without opening it. As far as Justin knew, it had just been sitting there ever since.

Justin sat down on the edge of his bed and stared at the BMX racing posters on his wall. He looked at the jar of pennies on top of his dresser, the band T-shirts that were piled up in his closet. His room was the same as it always was: dark blue-and-red walls. Same old furniture. Stupid posters and pictures he'd ripped out of magazines.

Justin walked downstairs and into the kitchen. The house was empty and silent. The only sound was the air-conditioning trying to combat the brutal Texas heat. His mom was at the grocery store, and his dad was back at work. She'd begged him to take some time off after the funeral, but he'd just muttered something about "keeping the business running," and headed out to his truck. It didn't surprise Justin that his dad wanted to stay busy—he wasn't the type to sit around and think about things.

Justin opened the refrigerator and poked around inside. He wasn't hungry—he hadn't been for days. He was just bored. He turned on the giant television in the living room and flipped around a few stations.

There was nothing good on. He shut it off again and tossed the remote onto the couch. Even if he had a cell phone and could text anyone, there was no one that he wanted to talk to . . . besides Kyle.

★ ★ ★

THE BEDROOM DOOR SQUEAKED A LITTLE AS JUSTIN eased it open. He stepped into his brother's room and shut the door behind him. The room was cold after being closed up with the air-conditioning running for days on end. Justin felt weird standing there by himself, as though he was intruding. It wasn't like someone was going to catch him there. Kyle was gone. His mother hadn't been inside the room for weeks, preferring to leave it exactly as it was before Kyle had left. His father just pretended the room didn't exist. No surprise there, either.

Kyle's room had always been neat. Neater than Justin's room anyway. It was almost like Kyle had been an organized Marine from the time he was a kid. The covers were pulled up snugly on his bed. The corners of the sheet and blanket were tucked firmly under the mattress. His books were lined up like little soldiers on the shelves. The football and basketball posters on his walls were perfectly straight. The top of his dresser was bare, except for a pair of cuff links he wore to his senior prom and four framed photos: all four Wincotts at Kyle's Marine Corps boot camp graduation; Kyle and his best friend, Tyler, at a party in high school, their arms across each other's shoulders; a shot of Kyle and Max posing side by side; and Justin and Kyle as kids, sitting in a giant cardboard box together.

Justin walked over to the footlocker. The large, rectangular plastic chest rested at the foot of Kyle's bed. It suddenly occurred to Justin that the harder he tried not to think about Kyle or Max, the more they fought their way into his brain. He had never really stopped thinking about them—Max especially, since the funeral.

Justin knelt down in front of the footlocker, lifted the latch, and eased open the lid. It was as neatly organized as Kyle's room. A pile of worn cotton workout clothes—soft T-shirts and sweatpants—rested next to a stack of camouflage fatigues and a massive pile of socks. Marines must use a ton of socks, Justin figured, as he thought about how sweaty his feet got just doing normal stuff like riding his BMX bike for a few hours.

There were other things in the box—a creased notebook filled with Kyle's handwriting, a couple of novels, a few photographs—but Justin didn't feel like looking at those right now. He pushed them to the side and found a dog toy. It was a bright red rubber thing, round and smooth, like three circles stacked on top of one another. It was covered with Max's teeth marks and scratches.

It was solid and heavy in his hand, and he hefted it up and down a couple of times. Justin couldn't picture the deranged dog he'd met at the church chewing happily on a dog toy. Gnawing off a grown man's arm, maybe, but nothing as normal as playing with a plain old piece of rubber. He dropped it back in the bottom of the footlocker with a thunk, and something shiny caught his eye. He pushed aside a couple of canvas belts and an empty backpack, and found a long metal chain underneath. He lifted it up slowly.

Somewhere in his gut he knew what it was before he saw the lightweight metal rectangles with rounded corners dangling from the end—Kyle's dog tags. Justin held them in his hand and read the stamped letters that spelled out his brother's full name, his date of birth, his religion—all the information the Marines would need to confirm his identity if the worst-case scenario happened . . . no, *when* the worst-case scenario happened, Justin thought angrily.

The tags jingled in Justin's hand. He didn't hear the door open behind him.

"Lot to learn from in there."

Justin jumped at the sound of his dad's voice. He didn't sound mad that Justin was in Kyle's room, but Justin felt weird about being found in there all the same.

"About what?" Justin asked, his voice completely neutral. He kept his eyes on the trunk in front of him.

"Being a man," his dad said. The back of Justin's neck turned red and the blood rushed to his ears as his temper flared, but he fought to contain his anger.

Justin calmly placed the dog tags back into the bottom of the locker, next to the rubber toy, and snapped the locker shut. He stood up and faced his dad. Suddenly, he couldn't keep his fury in anymore—his dad had no idea what "being a man" meant.

"Being a man and enlisting and getting killed, like Kyle? Or being a man and getting my leg shot up, like you? Tell me what I'm supposed to learn from either of those things." Justin's heart pounded in his chest. His dad's eyes narrowed.

"When you talk about your brother," his father said quietly, his voice like steel, "you show some respect."

Justin stared his father straight in the face. He knew he was provoking his dad, but he didn't care. It was like scratching an itch—it wasn't going to fix anything, but it felt too good to stop.

"Show some respect? Is that how I prove myself to you?" Justin pushed even harder.

"Kyle never had to prove anything to anyone." The veins in his dad's temples throbbed as he spoke. "Especially not to me." His dad shook his hands at Justin, disgusted, then left Kyle's room.

Justin followed him toward the stairs, not ready to give up the fight just yet. No—he wanted to take this argument all the way, until his dad understood how much Justin blamed him for Kyle joining the Marines, for Kyle leaving—for Kyle getting killed.

"You actually think Kyle *wasn't* trying to prove himself to you?" Justin shouted at his dad's back. "Are you kidding me?"

His dad stopped in his tracks at the top of the stairs. He spun around so he was face-to-face with Justin.

Justin cut his dad off before he could speak. "All he ever *did* was try to prove himself to you!"

"Guys—" His mom's voice shot up from the bottom of the stairs.

"If he hadn't," Justin went on, ignoring his mom, "I bet he'd still be alive today."

His dad leaned in close to Justin's face. "What do you know about it?" His eyes locked on Justin's. "You've never put your life on the line for anything. Unless it was in some stupid video game."

"Guys!" his mom called again.

"You'd like me to get myself killed," Justin said, holding his dad's gaze. "Wouldn't you?"

His dad flinched, and Justin knew he'd hit a nerve. He thought it'd feel good, but instead he just felt sick to his stomach.

His mom ran up the stairs, clutching the cordless phone in her hand. "Guys—listen to me!" Both Justin and his dad turned to glare at her, identical looks of fury on their faces.

She held the phone out in front of her, a pleading look on her face. "Sergeant Reyes called. *They're going to kill Max.*"

FIVE

JUSTIN BARELY HAD TIME TO PUT ON HIS SHOES BEFORE hopping into the back of his dad's SUV. He clicked in his seat belt just as his dad threw the car into reverse and they screeched out of the driveway. His mom pulled directions up on her phone to the military kennel.

"He bit his handler," his mom explained. "Bad. And a couple of the other guys, too."

"Look, we'll go see him," his dad said, his hands gripping the steering wheel tightly. "But I'm not making any promises."

"I told Sergeant Reyes we'd take him in," his mom went on, ignoring his dad. "But he said Max was just too dangerous. I told him we were coming, and he said he'd see what he can do. But unless he can be convinced otherwise, they're putting him down tonight."

"Unless *I* can be convinced otherwise, I'm not putting my family at risk," Justin's dad said firmly.

His mom sat back in her seat and stared out the window.

"We can't let it happen," she said to her reflection.

★ ★ ★

THE SECOND JUSTIN OPENED HIS CAR DOOR, HE HEARD the deafening sound of barking dogs. So many dogs . . . so much barking. As Sergeant Reyes shook hands with his parents and gave Justin a nod, Justin took in the large, nondescript building in front of him. Justin was surprised that the world-famous military dog training facility, Maitland, was so normal-looking.

"Dogs can have post-traumatic stress disorder, just like people can," Reyes explained as they followed him around the side of the building. "When Max lost his trainer—when he lost Kyle—he lost his anchor."

The group stopped on the edge of a dirt training area surrounded by a chain link fence. Justin watched a dog run at top speed toward a trainer wearing a puffy full-body suit. The man wore extra pads on his arms and legs, and he bent his knees a little, preparing for the dog to attack him. Justin knew it was just a practice exercise, but he had never seen a dog with such power and control in his body—it was actually pretty impressive.

"Max bonded so closely with Kyle," Reyes said as they watched the exercise. "They ate, slept, fought together—it's proving hard to get him to follow orders from anyone else."

Justin heard his mom suck in her breath as the dog launched himself at the trainer. The dog flashed his teeth and gums just before his mighty jaw clamped down on the man's padded arm. Justin swallowed hard. The dog began wrenching his head around violently, pulling the trainer with him.

Reyes nodded toward the scene they were witnessing. "That's nine hundred pounds of pressure coming down on that arm."

Justin's dad let out a quiet whistle. He and Reyes exchanged a knowing glance.

"That's why we're reluctant to adopt out a problem dog," Reyes said. "Someone could really get hurt. Or worse."

"Let's see Max," Justin's mom said. It was the voice

she used when she didn't want anyone to argue with her.

Justin walked behind Reyes as they stepped into the main building of Maitland. The barking was incredibly loud once they got inside. He could barely hear himself think as his eardrums vibrated with the sharp yelps of dozens of dogs. Justin took in the massive space. It was brightly lit and spotlessly clean. The walls were lined with tall chain-linked metal cages, each one big enough for a grown man, and each one containing a dog like Max. The dogs moved freely within them. Some lay down, resting, and some were hyper, jumping up and down and wagging their tails at the sight of Justin and his family.

Justin's stomach churned. He didn't know why he was nervous to see Max, and he wasn't even sure Max would remember him. Reyes led Justin and his parents down the long row of cages. The dogs followed them with their eyes as they passed. After what felt like an eternity, they finally stopped in front of Max's cage. Reyes made them stand back at a safe distance, about five feet away.

Justin's heart nearly broke in two at the sight of Max. While the other dogs were happy or relaxed, Max was neither. He wasn't barking or wagging his tail. He wasn't even watching them as they approached. Nope, Max lay curled up with his head on his paws. His eyes were partly open, but he wasn't looking at anything. He looked sad and alone, like he had nothing to live for. One ear flicked in Justin's direction, but otherwise Max showed no sign of recognition or excitement.

"He can't handle sharp noises anymore," Reyes said with a sigh. "Gunshots and explosions send him into a panic."

Justin studied Max's half-closed eyes and the way his body sighed with each breath. Justin had never imagined that it was possible to describe a dog this way, but Max looked like he'd just given up.

"These dogs are bred to work," Reyes went on. "Take that purpose away from them, and they're lost. Max can't serve anymore. And if he can't serve, he's a danger to people wherever he is."

Justin's mom let out a stifled cry and her eyes filled with tears. She shook her head as she looked at Max. When she spoke, Justin recognized the resolve in her voice. It was almost as if because she hadn't been able to save Kyle, she was determined to help Max.

"This family looks out for its own," she said.

Reyes studied her for a long moment before nodding. Though no one had explained it to him, he seemed to understand that Max was the closest thing Justin's family had to Kyle.

Reyes stepped closer to Max's cage. "How we doing, Max?" he asked, his voice soft.

With lightning speed, Max jumped up and snarled at Reyes, baring his teeth. The dog had moved so fast that Justin and his parents had leaped back in surprise. Max was no longer the forlorn, listless animal they had seen just seconds before. Now he was a wild beast—he scratched at the cage with his giant paws and growled at Sergeant Reyes as if he wanted to eat him whole. Max's eyes were filled with rage.

"It's okay, boy," Reyes said in a calming tone. "Sit, Max. Take it easy."

Max barked menacingly. Reyes turned to Justin's parents and shook his head, as if to say there was nothing he could do to stop Max from meeting his fate—being put down.

His dad put a hand on his mom's arm. "Pam, honey—" he began.

Justin saw the pain in his mother's eyes and the worry on his father's face. Before he knew what he was doing, Justin took a deep breath and stepped toward Max's cage.

"Justin—" his dad and the sergeant said at the same time.

Justin ignored them. "Hey, Max," Justin said. "Remember me?" He inched another tiny step forward.

Max barked again, but he sounded less angry and afraid. He sniffed at the air and seemed to recognize Justin's scent. His growl trailed off.

"You sure you want to do this?" Reyes asked Justin. Justin wasn't sure, but he nodded. He had no idea what to do with a dog, but he couldn't bear seeing his mom so sad. If there was anything he could do to make her feel better, then he was going to do it—even if it meant losing a hand to an angry canine.

Reyes reached into his pocket and held something out to Justin. It was a rubber dog toy, like the one he'd found in Kyle's footlocker.

"It's called a Kong," Reyes said. "We use them in training. It's a reward."

"So I should give it to him?" Justin asked.

"If he earns it."

Justin nodded, his palms sweaty on the rubber toy.

"Go slow and steady," Reyes said as Justin shuffled

toward Max and held out the Kong. "No sudden moves."

Max let out a low growl and kept his eyes on the toy. Justin's parents watched anxiously. Justin exhaled and studied Max for any signs that he was going to go bonkers.

"Check it out, Max," Justin said evenly. "Cool toy, right?"

Still standing, Max pressed his nose against the cage and sniffed at the toy. He tilted his head to one side inquisitively, his ears rotating forward, as if he was trying to ask a question.

"How do I get him to sit?" Justin called over his shoulder.

"I think right now you'd better concentrate on giving him that Kong and keeping your hand attached to your wrist," Reyes said.

Justin kept his gaze locked on the dog. "Very funny. Seriously. What's the hand signal?" Justin turned his head ever so slightly toward Reyes and watched him as he demonstrated the command. Justin looked back at Max and took a deep breath. He made an upright fist with his free hand and held it against his chest. "Sit," he said as firmly as he could—all while trying to hide his utter terror that Max was going to bust through the bars and attack him.

Max flinched at the sound of Justin's voice, but he stayed standing.

Justin repeated the hand gesture. "Sit!" he commanded.

Max sat, his eyes glued to the Kong.

Justin's mom gasped. His dad exhaled. Reyes let out a surprised "Huh." Justin couldn't believe that it had worked.

"Here you go, psycho hound," Justin said as he slowly nudged the Kong through the bars of the cage. Justin could see Max tensing up as the toy got closer to his snout. All of a sudden, Max lunged forward. Justin braced himself for the horrible sensation of Max's jaws tearing into his flesh, but nothing happened. Max wrapped his mouth around the Kong and gently tugged it from Justin's grip.

Justin couldn't help but smile. Without thinking, he reached the tips of his fingers through the cage to pet Max's head. He could feel Max's warm breath on his hand, but before he made contact, a protective growl rumbled from the dog's throat. Justin gave an anxious smile and snatched his hand away from the cage. Max backed up and lay down, the Kong tucked between his two front paws. He got to work chewing as hard as he could, his ears perked up and happy.

"Right, sorry," Justin said. "You enjoy that Kong. I'll be over here."

Reyes put a firm hand on Justin's shoulder. "That was impressive, son," he said. The look on his face was a combination of awe and respect.

Justin looked at his parents, not sure what would happen next.

"Well," his dad said, "I guess we'll be taking Max home, Sergeant."

SIX

JUSTIN'S DAD POUNDED A METAL STAKE INTO THE grass in their backyard. Max flinched every time the rubber mallet made contact, but Justin held him firmly on a short leash. The sun was high in the sky, and the late afternoon was unbearably hot and humid. Justin was melting, and he couldn't imagine how Max felt in his heavy black and tan coat. Then Justin remembered that Afghanistan was probably even hotter, and Max was trained to endure those insane temperatures.

Max had been agitated but not aggressive on the ride home. Reyes had loaned them a cage to use in their car, and Max had turned circles while they drove. But he hadn't growled or barked that much, which was a good sign. Now that they'd gotten Max home, though, Justin wasn't really sure what they were supposed to do with him. It wasn't like he was a lapdog like Chuy's twenty Chihuahuas. Sure, Max had been Kyle's sidekick, but that didn't make him safe to have inside.

"I hate to tie him up in the backyard like this," Justin's mom said over the banging of the mallet.

His dad stopped his work for a moment and looked at his wife. "Pamela, we talked about this. He's too unstable to keep in the house, and we can't just let him run around out here, either. What if he got out of the yard? He'll be fine."

"Why don't you just put up a fence?" Justin asked.

His dad spun around to look at him, his neck darkening in the sun. "And who's going to pay for that? You?"

"No, but if you do, I'll trick the neighborhood kids into whitewashing it," Justin joked.

"You're hilarious." His dad turned back to his mom. "You sure this one's ours?"

She grinned back at him. "I've got the stretch marks to prove it."

Justin's dad chuckled and gave the stake one last

blow. Justin couldn't remember the last time he'd heard his father laugh—or his mom make a joke. He also couldn't remember the last time his dad had gone to this much trouble for something that mattered to him. He would only take in a potentially man-eating dog for Kyle. Never for Justin. Figured.

His dad pulled on the stake and seemed satisfied that it would stay in the ground, no matter how hard Max pulled. He looped a long piece of metal chain through it and took one step toward Max, ready to fasten the chain to his collar. Max snarled and lowered himself into a crouch, pulling on his leash. Justin's dad jumped backward and quickly retracted his hand.

"Here," his dad said, thrusting the chain at Justin. "You do it."

Justin didn't feel like arguing with his dad; he just wanted to do whatever would get him back to his normal life. He took the leash and, without a word, leaned over and slowly, gently, quietly snapped it onto Max's collar. Max plopped down onto the ground as if he'd been living in their backyard his whole life. The dog looked completely relaxed. His tongue lolled out of his mouth and he panted a little. It was almost as if he'd just pretended to be crazy earlier—like he was messing with them or something.

"All right, then," his mom said, sounding amused. "Looks like he's all settled."

Justin did a quick calculation and figured he had enough time for a quick bike ride before it got too dark. He stood up to leave.

"Justin," his mom said, "let's go in and fix Max's dinner."

Justin stopped, shook his head, and held both hands up in front of him. A flash of anger shot through him.

"Whoa, wait a minute," Justin said, backing away from his parents and Max. "I helped you get him here, but I—" Max jumped back up and started to growl at Justin, suspicious of all the sudden movement and the anger in Justin's tone. He lowered his voice. "But I did not sign on to take care of Kyle's crazy dog."

His dad may have been laughing just a moment before, but he definitely wasn't amused anymore. He put down the rubber mallet and looked down at the ground for a moment, collecting his thoughts. Then he lifted himself to his feet with some effort and limped toward Justin. His mom watched them from across the yard, worry on her face.

"Kyle is gone." His dad's eyes glinted with anger

as he spoke. "So Max isn't Kyle's dog anymore. He's yours. Have I made myself clear?"

Justin ground his teeth together. He held his dad's gaze but didn't say anything. What was the point? His dad cared more about a stupid dog that had once belonged to Kyle than he did about his own living, breathing son. There was no point in fighting about it—his dad was never going to change.

After a long pause, Justin pushed past his dad and stomped toward the house. He could hear Max's chain rattling as the dog hopped up and tried to follow him.

"Sit!" his dad snapped at Max. Max barked, and his dad muttered under his breath.

Justin heard Max whimpering as he slammed the back door behind him. He stormed into the kitchen, grabbed the ten-pound bag of dry dog food from the floor and ripped it open. He snatched up the new stainless steel bowl and knelt on the ground, reaching his hand into the giant bag. The food smelled gross—he nearly gagged. His mom stepped through the back door and leaned against the kitchen counter, her arms crossed. Justin shot her a glare as he dumped a pile of kibble into the bowl with a loud rattle, then wiped his hand on his jeans.

"Justin."

Justin ignored his mom and added another handful of food. He had to admit it wasn't as bad the second time.

"*Justin*," she said again.

Justin turned to his mom. "What?" he asked. He knew he was pushing his luck with his tone, but he couldn't help himself. He was too mad—but about what, he couldn't exactly say.

"Justin, listen to me." His mom's voice was firm but understanding. "Your brother loved you so much. More than you'll ever know. You get that, right?"

Hot tears sprang to Justin's eyes. He turned away so his mom couldn't see them.

"If that's true then he wouldn't have been in such a rush to take off and leave me here to deal with Dad all by myself."

"Your father loves you, too, Justin. So much." She sighed and let out a little cluck of her tongue. "It's just—none of you Wincott boys ever figured out a way to tell each other that."

A hard lump formed in Justin's throat, and he couldn't speak. He didn't know what to say anyway. His dad certainly hadn't ever figured out a way to tell Justin he loved him. Seemed like his dad had mostly just let Justin know how disappointed he was.

Justin's mom stepped forward and dropped her arms to her sides. "In case you're interested in changing that, your mom could sure use a hug right about now," she said.

Justin stood up and stepped forward, wrapping her in a tight hug.

"My goodness, Justin," she said, pulling back to look at him for a second. "You're officially as tall as I am now." She shook her head and squeezed him close again.

Over her shoulder, Justin looked through the kitchen window and saw his dad standing in the yard, watching them. Max lay on the ground behind him. His dad's brow was tightly knit and his lips were pressed firmly together. Justin was surprised to see that his dad looked like he was struggling to keep his emotions in check. They held each other's gaze for a moment, then his dad gave Justin a quick—almost invisible—nod before looking away.

★ ★ ★

A SHARP, DESPERATE WAIL PIERCED THE NIGHTTIME quiet. *Max.*

That dog had been barking his head off for hours. So much for the happy, mellow Max.

Justin rolled over in his bed and pulled a pillow

across his head. He held the cushion firmly against his ear, but he could still hear Max's howling.

The noise stopped for a millisecond. Justin released his grip on the pillow, but before he could even get his hopes up, the growling and barking started right up again. It shifted from a deep bass to a high-pitched whine and back again.

Justin kept his eyes shut, but sleep was impossible. There was no way Max could possibly keep this up all night, he thought. Right?

"*JUSTIN!*"

His dad's angry voice boomed from down the hall. He was not a man who liked to have his sleep interrupted.

"Get out there and quiet that dog down!"

Justin let out a frustrated groan and hurled the pillow across the room. It rattled his dresser and slid to the ground with a soft *plonk*.

Why is this my problem? he wanted to shout back at his dad. *He isn't even my dog.*

But Justin kept his mouth shut and stomped over to his bedroom door. He flung it open, not bothering to stop it from smacking into the wall. Justin moved past his parents' room and down the hall to Kyle's room.

He was so irritated—and distracted by the yelping and howling outside—that for a moment, he almost forgot. He was about to knock on his brother's door . . . but there was no need to knock.

Justin wrapped his hand around Kyle's doorknob. Kyle, who would know how to get his dog to shut up. Kyle, who had gone to Afghanistan with Max by his side. Only one of them had come home alive—and that one was in the backyard barking for attention in the middle of the night. And there was no one to give it to him but Justin.

Max's lonely cries echoed in the backyard. Justin could hear his parents through the wall, speaking in a harsh whisper. He stepped into Kyle's darkened bedroom, flicked on the light, and knelt down by the footlocker on the floor. He wrapped his fingers around the Kong.

"Justin—are you gonna shush that dog?" his dad yelled.

Justin ignored him again and went downstairs. He crossed the darkened living room and kitchen, stepping through the back door and into the cool evening air. The yard was lit by the nearly full moon, which hung bright and high in the sky. At the sound of the door sliding open, Max's black snout shot toward Justin, and his eyes glinted in the moonlight. He stopped mid-bark. It was suddenly so quiet that Justin could hear the dog's name tag jingling against his collar. After all that noise, the silence was precious.

Justin stood in his pajama pants and sweatshirt, the grass poking at his bare feet, not completely sure what he should do. He held the Kong behind his back and took a step toward Max. Max watched Justin approach, his eyes shadowed and wary. Justin thought the dog looked sad, then shook the thought out of his head. Max was a million times better off than he had been this morning in the kennel, so why was he so upset?

"You gonna stop that freakin' noise now?" Justin said. His voice sounded louder than he meant it to. Max's wet nose twitched. Justin took another couple of steps forward, and the dog let out a low, soft whimper. Justin got closer, and suddenly Max started barking again, the sound ricocheting off the house and vibrating in Justin's eardrums. Dogs from around the neighborhood responded with excited barks of their own.

"Oh come *on*," Justin grumbled. Max snapped his mouth shut with a little clack of his teeth. He whimpered once and did a nervous dance with his feet. His nails dug into the grass.

Justin held the Kong out in front of him. Max's eyes grew round with excitement as he studied the toy, his ears rising slowly in sharp peaks. Justin made the "sit" gesture Reyes had taught him.

"Sit," he commanded.

Max barked, a minor complaint.

Justin repeated the hand motion. "Sit."

Max sat. Justin tried to play it cool, but he couldn't believe it had actually worked. Justin slowly raised the Kong toward Max's nose. "Easy, boy. Easy . . ."

Max stretched his snout out gingerly, taking quick short breaths through his nose. Every muscle in his body tensed, as if he were poised to attack the enemy or discover a cache of weapons.

Boy and dog stayed perfectly still for a brief moment, suspended in a state of mutual longing—Justin for quiet, Max for the Kong.

"Attaboy," Justin whispered.

Max's eyes remained locked on the red toy as he brought his mouth ever so slightly closer to it. Finally, his muzzle rested against the smooth rubber. He opened his mouth slowly, and gently closed his teeth around the Kong. Justin pulled his hand away as Max began chomping, loud and hard.

"Good boy, Max," Justin said softly, still trying not to spook the dog. Justin wasn't sure it was a good idea, but he couldn't resist: He reached out his hand to pet Max's head. "Good boy."

Without even looking in Justin's direction, Max ducked and jerked his head away before Justin could touch him. The dog scooted backward and dropped to the ground, where he lay on his belly and maneuvered the Kong with his mouth and two front paws. Justin took a step backward.

"Looks like you're cool now, Max," he said. "See you in the morning."

Justin walked back toward the house. Suddenly, he heard Max's long chain rattling, and the dog began barking and howling even louder than before. Justin spun around to see Max up on his back feet, straining forward against the chain, his collar tight around his throat.

"What is *wrong* with you, Max?"

In reply, Max stopped barking and sat down. Justin studied him for a long moment, not sure what to do, then shrugged and started to leave again. Max raised his nose toward the sky and let out a long, distressed howl. *AHWOOOOO.*

"*JUSTIN!*" his dad bellowed from inside the house.

"I'm trying!" Justin shouted over Max's wailing.

"Y'all shut that dog up," came a voice from the house next door. "You hear me, Wincott? Shut him up or I'm coming out with my .45!"

"Come on over, Mr. Hidalgo," Justin called back. "You'd be doing me a favor, seriously!"

The only response was the slamming of the Hidalgos' window. Justin took that as a good sign.

The chorus of voices only upset Max more. He was back up on his hind legs, pulling harder against the chain, barking frantically. Justin's nerves were shot, his ears were ringing, and he just wanted the sound to stop—he wanted it *all* to stop. He just wanted life to return to the way it was before Kyle left. Before Kyle died. Before Max came to live with them. He squeezed his eyes shut and balled his hands into fists. The barking pounded into his head.

Justin opened his eyes.

"What do you *want*, Max?" he asked through gritted teeth. He took a step toward the dog.

Max stopped barking.

A thought occurred to Justin, and he backed away. Max let out a low growl. Justin stepped forward again. Max went silent, his eyes big and hopeful.

"No way. You—you want me to stay?" Justin asked. He shook his head and let out a laugh. "I'm not staying out here with you. My bed's in there." He jerked a thumb in the direction of the house. "Sit, Max. Just—sit. Please."

Max sat and bowed his head a little. Justin tried to leave again, but Max's woeful whimpering stopped him in his tracks. Justin exhaled slowly, his shoulders sagging. There was no getting out of this—not if he wanted anyone in the entire neighborhood to get any sleep. He walked back to Max, who looked up at him expectantly.

"Fine," Justin said, flopping down onto the grass, but keeping a few feet between him and Max. "But I can't stay here all night. Just until you fall asleep." They stared at each other as they came to an understanding. "Okay?"

Max lay back down on his belly and, tilting his head sideways, snatched up the Kong with the side of his mouth.

"Right. Okay," Justin said.

Max paid Justin no mind as he got to work on his chew toy. *Great,* Justin thought. *So I'll sit here on the wet grass instead of in my warm bed, and you'll just ignore me.* Justin ripped up a handful of grass and poked at it in his palm. The night surrounded him. The only sound was the gnawing of Max's teeth against the rubber, which was now coated in thick slobber. Justin lay back and stared up at the moon and the thin clouds painted against the dark sky.

I'll just lie here for a minute, he thought as sleep took over.

★ ★ ★

SOMETHING PAINFULLY BRIGHT WAS SHINING AGAINST his eyelids. Justin opened his eyes and squinted into the flat morning sun.

"What the—"

He sat up and looked around, confused. His head was pounding, and his neck and back were stiff. The day was already hot. Max sat just inches away, his paws lined up straight out in front of him, his ears pricked up and his eyes on Justin. *Like he's been watching me,* Justin thought.

"How long have I been asleep?" Justin asked. Max sniffed at him, his nose brushing almost imperceptibly against Justin's arm. Max exhaled sharply through his nostrils, his breath hot on Justin's skin.

"Justin? What are you doing out here?"

Justin whipped his head around to see his mom standing in her pink bathrobe.

"I've been looking all over for you. Have you been out here all night?" she called from the doorway.

Justin glanced at Max, who put his head down on his paws, as if he could finally get some rest after a long night's watch. Max's tail thumped gently against the grass.

"No. I mean, yeah, I guess. Sort of. I was just . . . hanging out with Max," Justin said to his mom.

A huge grin broke out on her face. "Looks like you could use some pancakes." She stepped back inside the house. Justin could see her moving around the kitchen. He stretched his arms over his head and looked down at Max. "You must be hungry, too, boy."

Max just gazed up at him with his big brown eyes.

Mom stuck her head out the kitchen window.

"I almost forgot," she said. "Chuy called. He said it's urgent."

SEVEN

THE HOUSES ON EITHER SIDE OF THE STREET PASSED BY in a blur as Justin raced by on his bike. He pedaled harder, reaching the edge of his neighborhood and turning down a wide gravel path that led into the thick green woods. Justin always loved the way it instantly got quiet when he hit the dirt path that wound through the trees. He cruised along the familiar trail, where he knew every curve and tree root. He pumped his legs and took some air as he sailed over bumps and dips.

Justin had barely seen Chuy since Kyle's funeral, and he knew that his friend was desperate to see him. The funny thing was, Justin was pretty excited to see him, too, which was way different than how he'd felt yesterday. Justin wondered if Max had anything to do with it. Maybe he should always sleep outside on the ground?

He could hear the voices of his friends before he reached the big opening in the trees. A large curved ramp made of reclaimed wooden fences circled the makeshift bike park. He watched as a bunch of kids on their bikes raced along the ramp's edge, pushing one another to go even faster. He could already hear Chuy's laugh as he joked with all the other bikers.

Justin pulled into the clearing and slammed on his brakes, sending a cloud of dirt into the air. It was still morning, but the day was already humid and sticky.

A few heads turned in Justin's direction.

"What's up, hombre?"

"Where you been, man?"

"Good to have you back, J."

Chuy skidded up to Justin on his bike and hopped off.

"Yo, you look like crap," Chuy said.

"Good morning to you, too." Justin rolled his eyes at his friend. Leave it to Chuy to notice that he'd spent the night using his backyard as a bed.

"Seriously, man, you look worse than my mom on my sister's prom night."

Justin shrugged. "I didn't get much sleep last night."

"You better work on your beauty rest," Chuy said.

"Is that why you called at the crack of dawn? To give me beauty tips?"

"No, man." Chuy dismissed Justin with a wave. "And sorry about calling your house."

"It's cool. Let me guess. Your cousin is all worked up because you never gave him this?" Justin pulled a slim plastic DVD case from his pocket and waved it in front of Chuy's face. Justin almost wanted to laugh at Chuy's comical sigh of relief.

"Dude, you took off like your pants were on fire when my dad showed up," Justin chuckled. "You could have stuck around for another thirty seconds."

"I'm not stupid enough to mess with a war hero, dude," Chuy said.

"What war hero, man?"

"Your dad. I hear he got his leg shot up in some crazy firefight in Vietnam."

Justin shook his head. "Iraq. But close enough."

Chuy didn't seem to hear him. He was too busy cocking his arms as if he were holding a machine gun.

He made a *rat-a-tat-tat* noise as he shot off a series of imaginary rounds.

"Yo, they should send *me* into a real fight," Chuy bragged. "I'll show them what a hero is."

"You're real cool under pressure, huh, Chuy?" a girl's voice came from behind them. Justin spun around to see a girl about his age leaning on the handlebars of a bike. He'd never seen her before. She was dressed in all black—black cutoff shorts, black high tops, a black My Chemical Romance T-shirt. Thick black bangs crossed her forehead. Even her heavy eyeliner was black. Under the eyeliner, she had huge brown eyes, which focused intently on Chuy, then on Justin.

"Shut it, Carmen," Chuy said.

Justin was confused. How did Chuy know this girl?

"Hi," she said to Justin.

"Uh, hi." Justin gave her a lame half wave, then instantly regretted it.

"This is my cousin," Chuy said with a disgusted nod toward Carmen.

Justin couldn't think of anything to say. Her dark eyes were still zeroed in on him, making his cheeks feel kind of hot. "You have a lot of cousins," he finally blurted out.

"Tell me about it." Chuy rolled his eyes, and Carmen shook her head at him, annoyed. "She's staying on my couch. I can't even watch TV anymore." Chuy leaned toward Justin and said in a loud whisper, "Her pops kicked her out."

"Chuy, stop making up stories," she said with an exasperated sigh.

"Is it true?" he asked. Carmen nodded. "What happened?"

She tugged on the collar of her T-shirt to reveal a fresh tattoo on the side of her neck. It was a small black dog paw. He had to admit that it looked pretty awesome against her tan skin. He also noticed that she had a few feathers woven into her dark hair. None of the girls at Justin's school dressed like she did. She looked way cooler—it was like she was Goth or punk or something.

"Nice," said Justin.

"We were eating dinner and my dad saw it," Carmen said. "He told me to get rid of it or he'd do it himself. So I handed him my knife and told him to go ahead. He just stood up, called my aunt—"

"My mom," Chuy interjected.

"And told her he didn't want to look at my face anymore," she finished. "So here I am."

"Lucky me," Chuy said. He crossed his skinny arms and rolled his eyes at her.

"Shut it, Chuy," Justin and Carmen said at the same time, then both laughed at the jinx.

Justin could see that Carmen was almost his height, and way taller than Chuy. His best friend always complained that he hadn't hit his growth spurt yet, and that he was going to be way taller than everyone in their class by the time summer break was over, but Justin wasn't so sure about that.

"I'm Carmen," she said.

"Yeah. I mean, I'm Justin." He gave her a shy smile. Was he supposed to shake her hand or something?

Chuy looked back and forth between them. "I'm out," he said with a sigh, pocketing the burned CD. He picked up his bike off the ground and pushed it toward the ramp. "You gonna ride with us?" he called back over his shoulder.

"Can't," Justin said. "I have to go take care of the dog."

Chuy stopped and turned back to Justin, his eyebrows raised. He ran a hand through his curly hair, making it stick up even taller and messier.

"Yo, that's right. I heard you got your brother's crazy war dog. My cousin Felix works at the church. He said that dog tore up a whole bunch of Marines and put them in the hospital."

Justin held up a hand to stop Chuy from talking. "He didn't put anyone in the hosp—"

"You have an MWD?" Carmen interrupted, a look of surprise on her face.

"How do you know about MWDs?" Justin asked. He barely even knew what it meant, so how did Carmen know?

"She's really into dogs," Chuy answered for her. "She's like the dog whisperer."

Carmen ignored Chuy and stepped right in front of him, blocking his view of Justin. Chuy tried to scoot around her, but she kept moving, like a defensive basketball player protecting the net. "What kind?" she asked Justin.

"What kind of what?" Justin peered around her to look at Chuy, who wore an expression of sheer irritation. Carmen, on the other hand, was grinning from ear to ear, clearly enjoying messing with Chuy. Justin chuckled. He couldn't deny that it was sort of satisfying to see Carmen tormenting his friend.

"Your dog? What breed is he?" Carmen asked, while Chuy hopped up and down behind her.

Finally, Chuy faked her out and slipped in front of her.

"He's not really my . . ." Justin trailed off. He wasn't sure how much Chuy had told her about his family. About Kyle. "He's kind of like a German shepherd, but with a black face." He waved a hand in front of his own face to indicate Max's snout, then realized how dorky that must have looked and let his hand drop.

"Belgian Malinois," Carmen said with a firm nod. She put her hands on her hips. "Cool dog."

"Actually, Chuy's kind of right . . ." Justin said.

Chuy threw up his hands and mumbled, "Finally, someone acknowledges the truth around here."

"Max is totally crazy," Justin went on. "He won't let anyone near him but me. And he won't even let *me* touch him."

"Just be patient with him," Carmen replied. "He'll come around. Sounds like he's been through a lot."

"Yeah, I guess he has," Justin said. So Chuy *had* told her about Max and Kyle. Justin wasn't sure how he felt about that. People were going to treat him differently now that he'd lost his brother—he knew that—but he wished Carmen wasn't one of them.

A long look passed between Justin and Carmen. She

did seem cool, and he wanted to trust her. He needed all the help he could get with Max, but the last thing he wanted was for anyone—Carmen in particular—to help him because they felt sorry for him. He was not down with a pity party.

"She's like a Cesar Millan if Cesar Millan were a chick," Chuy said, breaking the silence. "She's even got the mustache to prove it."

In the blink of an eye, Carmen lashed out and swatted at Chuy, who hopped on his bike and pedaled away from her. He stopped just out of her reach. She looked back at Justin and rolled her eyes about her cousin. Justin laughed.

"If you need some help with him—the dog, not Chuy, I mean—I can come by and teach you a few tricks," Carmen said.

Chuy's head snapped around and his mouth hung open, as if he couldn't believe what he was hearing. He gave a low whistle. "What? Did she just invite herself over to—"

"Sure, uh . . . why not," Justin replied quickly.

Chuy's head shot around the other direction, and he gaped at his friend. "What? Did you just say she could—"

"How about later this afternoon?" Carmen said. "So I have time to cook up some treats for him? Like, three o'clock?"

"Cool," Justin said, but the word sort of got stuck in his throat. He didn't know why his face suddenly felt hot, but he had an overriding urge to turn his bike around and get out of there as quickly as possible. He hoped Carmen was as good with dogs as she said she was—he didn't want Max to go crazy on her. It'd be his butt on the line if she got hurt.

He jumped back on his bike and pedaled off in one direction, while Carmen rode off in another. Chuy looked completely abandoned.

"Dude—" Chuy shouted after Justin as he sped off. "What the heck just happened?"

Justin answered with a backward wave over his shoulder. It was a good question—what *had* just happened?

EIGHT

JUSTIN STOOD IN FRONT OF THE MIRROR AND RAN HIS fingers through his hair. Again. He looked down at his T-shirt and decided that it wasn't the right one to wear. Again. He pulled it over his head and was just about to change into a new one—Pink Floyd, *Dark Side of the Moon*—when he heard Max barking ferociously outside.

Justin stepped to his bedroom window and looked out, only to discover that Carmen and Chuy were standing right below his room. They looked up to see Justin framed in his window, shirtless. Justin wanted to hide—or maybe completely disappear—but it was too late. Chuy let out a wolf whistle, and Carmen just grinned.

Justin grimaced in embarrassment. He ducked down below the window frame and slipped on his shirt. Max was barking like mad in the yard. Justin hurried downstairs, crossed through the house and slid open the back door. Carmen and Chuy had stayed a few feet away from Max—just beyond the reach of his chain.

Carmen cast a sideways glance at Justin's T-shirt as he crossed the yard.

"Pink Floyd?" she teased. "You're one of those deep ones, huh?"

"What? They're the original emo." He couldn't stop himself from grinning. He ran a nervous hand through his hair, pushing his spikey bangs away from his eyes. Then he turned back to the barking monster that was tied up in his yard.

"It's okay, Max," Justin said as gently as he could. He took a few steps toward the dog. "It's okay, buddy. These are my friends." He held out the Kong, but Max just kept snarling and snapping. "Take it easy, buddy." What he really wanted to say was "Please don't eat my friends. Especially not the pretty one," but he managed to keep that to himself.

"Dude, that dog reminds me of your dad," Chuy said with an exaggerated shudder. He obviously wanted nothing to do with Max.

"Maybe this was a bad idea," Justin said. He backed away from the dog and stood close to Carmen and Chuy. He knew that Kyle had loved Max, and that they had watched each other's backs. He got that there *could* be a strong bond between a guy and his dog—he just didn't see how that was going to happen between him and Max. Justin wasn't Kyle, and that had always been the problem.

"Nah," Carmen said, her eyes focused on Max. She shook the paper sack in her hand and got down on one knee. The bag looked heavy and smelled delicious—Justin got a whiff of whatever Carmen had made. Max must have smelled it, too, because his barking slowed and he raised his nose to sniff at the air.

"Hey, Max," Carmen said in a super-friendly voice. "I made you some carnitas." She reached into the bag and pulled out a chunk of cooked pork. "You like home cooking?" Max responded by twitching his nose and barking again. But Justin thought that *this* bark sounded more curious and less rabid. Carmen waved the meat in front of Max, but kept her distance. "Smells good, right?"

Max snapped his mouth shut and whimpered a little.

Carmen took a step toward the dog.

"I wouldn't get any closer," Justin said. He moved forward so he could get between Carmen and Max if he needed to.

But Carmen didn't seem worried about what the dog might do. She was totally relaxed as she kept her eyes firmly on Max.

"This is close enough," she said in a soothing voice. "Let's let him think about it for a minute."

Justin couldn't believe his eyes: It really did look like Max was debating whether to keep barking or try for some food. His lips curled up in a gesture that meant he was ready to bite into something, but whether he wanted people or food was still unclear.

"Yo, guys, I'm out of here," Chuy said, throwing his hands in the air and taking a giant step backward. "That dog scares me. Carmen, I hope he doesn't bite you, but if he does, it's not my fault, right?"

"You don't have to leave, Chuy," Justin said, suddenly alarmed at the idea of being alone with Carmen. "Hang out. He won't hurt you."

"Nah, thanks, man. Between that dog and your mean old man, I don't want to be here anyway.

Nothing personal." Chuy cast a nervous look toward the house.

"My dad's at work," Justin said.

Carmen shot Chuy a sideways glance, then turned to Justin. "Why are you letting Chuy hate on your dad like that?"

Justin shrugged.

"I can say whatever I want about my dad," Carmen said, her eyebrows shooting up and her expression serious, "but if someone else disrespects him, that's not cool. That's called loyalty."

"That's called *crazy*," Justin said. "You and Max should get along just great."

Carmen shook her head at the boys. "I'm not the one he has to get along with." She handed Justin the carnita and nodded in Max's direction. "He's waited long enough."

Justin took the cooked meat and studied it. "How'd you get to be such an expert anyway?" he asked, worried that this might not be the best way to train Max. "I mean, do you have credentials or something—"

Carmen cut him off. "You going to eat that, or are you going to give it to your dog?" she asked. "'Cause he's waiting for you."

Max was definitely waiting—and it didn't look like his patience was going to last much longer. His eyes were locked on the food, and his whole head moved to follow it every time Justin's hand shifted even an inch.

Justin swallowed hard. He faced Max head-on and made the sit gesture with his free hand. "Sit."

Max sat.

At least that's one thing he can do, Justin thought. Max looked at Justin expectantly and licked his chops. Justin could see pools of drool in the corners of Max's mouth.

Nervously, Justin stretched out his hand in front of him and held the meat in front of Max's nose. Max snatched it from his hand—not aggressively, just excitedly. He chomped it down in a few firm chews.

"Look at that," Carmen said softly. "First time you had Mexican cooking, boy?" She took another piece of food from the bag and knelt down in front of Max. Justin and Chuy watched her carefully, unsure of what the dog would do. Was Carmen about to end up as a dog chew toy?

But Max reached out his snout and gently took the meat from her hand. He dropped it onto the ground in front of him and proceeded to lick it clean, then gulp down what was left. Carmen handed Justin another piece. "Now don't give it to him until he lets you touch him, okay?"

Justin nodded. "Okay."

He steeled himself and raised the meat toward Max's twitching nose. Max didn't take his eyes off the food. While Max waited for his treat, Justin reached his other hand up and out toward Max's head. Justin's heart pounded in his chest. In Justin's limited experience, Max had a way of being great for a few minutes, then losing his mind for no obvious reason. There was a fair chance he'd decide in a heartbeat that the carnitas weren't good enough and he wanted to snack on human flesh instead.

Justin's hand inched closer to Max's furry head, the meat almost at his mouth. It was like playing the hardest level on a video game, where you had to complete a dangerous task, fight off three enemies, keep an eye on your energy level, and not die, all at the same time.

"Don't do it, man!" Chuy cried out abruptly. Max, Justin, and Carmen all jumped at once. Justin pulled back his hand and Max growled a little.

"Ugh, Chuy!" Carmen exclaimed. She scrunched up her face and made a throat-slitting gesture at him.

"Are you trying to get my friend killed, Carmen?" Chuy complained.

"Just the opposite. I'm trying to keep him alive."

Justin had lost his nerve—he didn't want to pet Max anymore. "Maybe I should just give him the food first," he said to Carmen.

"No." Carmen shook her head firmly. "It's a reward. You don't get a reward if you haven't done anything to deserve it."

Justin's stomach churned. He didn't want to do this anymore, but deep down he knew Carmen was right. If Max was going to stick around, then Justin needed to be able to train him. Because if he couldn't, if Max remained too dangerous to be around other people, then Justin's parents would be forced to take him back to the kennel, where he would definitely be put down. Justin felt as if Max's very life depended on him, and he wouldn't be able to live with himself if anything happened to the dog that Kyle had loved. No. Justin couldn't give up on Max, even if he was afraid of him.

For the first time, Justin found himself wondering—if *he* was this nervous, then what was Max feeling? Maybe there really was a reason for Max's outbursts—Justin just hadn't been paying attention to them.

Justin turned back to the dog and focused again. He held the carnita out in one hand and reached out with the other. Keeping his eyes on the food, Max let Justin's fingers brush against the soft fur on the top of his head, then ducked away.

Just a touch, but it was something.

"Good job. Good boy, Max." Justin held the carnita out in front of him, and Max took it from him carefully, devouring it in two delicate bites. His tail rose up behind him. It wasn't quite a wag, but close. Justin exhaled and shook out his arms. He heard Chuy let out a big sigh, as though he'd been holding his breath.

"It's a start," Carmen said. They stood and watched Max nose at the ground, as if he hoped he might find a stray chunk of meat that he'd missed. "Do you have a leash?"

Justin nodded.

★ ★ ★

JUSTIN COULDN'T BELIEVE WHAT HE WAS SEEING. IF someone had tried to tell him earlier that Max would be on a leash by dinnertime, he would have laughed. But there was Max, clipped onto a leather strap, being led around the yard in a circle by Carmen.

She left very little slack on the line. Max walked

close to her side, and whenever he tried to pull ahead, Carmen jerked it back and commanded "Heel!" Sure enough, Max dropped back and returned to a slower pace.

"Wow," Chuy said.

"You can say that again," Justin replied.

"Wow." Chuy stuck out his tongue and put his hands up under his chin, as if he was a dog waiting for a treat.

"Ha, good boy, Chuy," Justin joked.

"You don't let your dog walk you," Carmen said to Justin as she turned back toward the boys. "You walk your dog." Carmen stopped, and Max stopped with her. "Stay," she ordered him. Max stayed. Carmen held out her end of the leash to Justin. "Your turn."

Justin forced himself not to hesitate. He took the leash and pulled Max in close to his side.

"Remember—dogs run in packs," Carmen said as Justin and Max began making a slow circle around the yard. "So if he leads you, he's leading the pack. He'll never listen to you if he thinks he's the leader."

Justin nodded, but he didn't want to speak. He could feel Max near his leg, walking in step with him. He didn't want to break their concentration. When Max started to move a little faster and get ahead of him, Justin jerked on the leash and Max fell back into rhythm with him. Was this how Kyle felt when he and Max went out on patrol—like he and the dog were totally in sync, practically a single unit?

A weird thought suddenly bubbled up in Justin's mind—a question so obvious, he was surprised it hadn't occurred to him before: If Max had always been by Kyle's side, no matter what, then how had Kyle gotten killed—and how had Max survived?

"He's picking this up really fast," Carmen said proudly, bringing Justin back from his thoughts.

Justin spoke without taking his eyes off Max. "My brother told us Max is a Specialized Search Dog. He could go out three hundred yards in front of his handler to search for explosives and weapons."

"You mean to tell me," Chuy cut in, "that we've got the Michael Jordan of dogs right here, and you've got him doing layups in your backyard?"

Justin paused, and Max stayed by his side. Justin held out the leash to Chuy. "You want to give it a go?"

Chuy shook his head. "Heck no. Are you crazy?"

"Didn't think so," Justin said with a smile.

Justin and Max continued their circle. Justin was so focused on the dog that he didn't notice when his mom came home and stood watching them from the kitchen window.

"All right, Max. You're such a superstar, huh?" Carmen said. "Let's see you work off the leash." She bent down and reached for the clasp on Max's collar.

"Whoa—I don't know," Justin said. "If anything happens, my dad will kill me."

"No pain, no gain," Carmen said. She looked up at Justin's worried face. "Nothing's going to happen. It's okay." Justin admired her confidence, even if he didn't entirely share it.

Carmen unhooked Max from the leash with a metallic *snap*. As if he'd received some kind of silent message, Max's whole demeanor changed. He suddenly crouched down, his whole body coiled tight like a spring—as if he were about to go searching for hidden weapons.

"See," Carmen said softly. "He knows what to do. Now walk with him, just like you did before."

"Heel." Justin took a few purposeful steps. Max stuck close to his side, just slightly behind him. Max's head was up, his ears pricked forward, and his eyes gleamed with focus. He seemed to be sniffing the ground and air with extra intensity. A squirrel skittered through the trees at the edge of the backyard, and Max's head snapped around so fast it was unbelievable. But he didn't run off after the animal—he stayed close to Justin's side and waited for his next command.

It was pretty cool to see Max in the search mode he'd been trained for. Kyle had always gone on and on about how Max could find anything, and Justin had usually rolled his eyes a little. *Max can do this, Max can do that.* It had always bugged Justin how his parents hung on to every word Kyle uttered about some dog they'd never even met. But now Justin was starting to understand why Kyle was so proud of Max—and why he and his unit had trusted Max with their lives.

Justin looked down at the dog, and Max looked back up at him. Justin smiled at Max, who panted in return.

Justin's mom stepped out into the backyard. "I don't believe what I'm seeing," she said. Justin froze. Max stood perfectly still at Justin's side. "How'd you get him to do that?"

"He already knew, ma'am," Carmen said politely. "We're just refreshing his memory."

"Mom, this is Carmen," Justin said, hoping that Max *and* his mom would stay on their best behavior. "Chuy's cousin. She's really good with dogs."

"I can see that."

"Nice to meet you, ma'am," Carmen said.

"Hi, Mrs. Wincott," Chuy mumbled, jamming his hands in his pockets.

"Hi, Chuy. It's a pleasure to meet you, Carmen."

"I was thinking we could give Max to her, Mom," Justin joked.

"No such luck, smart mouth." His mom turned to Chuy and Carmen with a smile. "You guys must have worked up quite an appetite out here. I'm about to make dinner if you'd like to join us."

Justin suddenly wanted to curl up in a little ball and hide—so much for good behavior. He couldn't believe his mom had just invited them to stay without clearing it with him first. He was afraid to look at Carmen. There was an awkward silence, then thankfully Chuy answered first.

"Thanks, but I need to go home," Chuy said, reading Justin's vibe. "You all have fun."

Justin held his breath, waiting to hear Carmen's reply. He didn't know if he wanted her to say yes or no.

"Thanks, Mrs. Wincott," Carmen said sweetly. "I'd be glad to."

NINE

JUSTIN COULDN'T MAKE EYE CONTACT WITH CARMEN. This was the most awkward dinner ever.

No one spoke. The room was silent, except for the scraping of knives and forks against plates. Justin couldn't help but think of Max all alone in the backyard, while the rest of them sat together inside. He let his mind drift back to their training session. Max had gotten even better by the end of the day, jogging alongside Justin in circles around the yard. When he'd fed Max dinner, the dog had happily scarfed it down—he'd worked up quite an appetite today with all that exercise. *At least someone was enjoying his dinner,* Justin thought bitterly.

“Please pass the potatoes,” his dad said from the head of the table without looking up. His mom cleared her throat from the other end.

Justin handed the bowl to his dad, who scooped a chunk onto his plate. Justin chewed and took a slug of his soda. He held the bottle up and tilted it toward Carmen. She nodded, and he refilled her cup. Still no one spoke. Justin stared at his food. It was so quiet that he heard the automatic ice maker in the freezer whirring and clicking, then dropping a load of ice cubes with a clatter.

“I’m sorry I burned the roast,” his mom blurted out. “I had it timed just perfectly, but then the phone rang, and it was Mary—” Out of nowhere, she began to cry. Tears pooled in her eyes and threatened to spill down her cheeks as she spoke. “And you know how Mary can just go on and on . . .” Her voice cracked and she put her head in her hands.

Justin considered crawling under the table, but he thought that might make things even worse for Carmen. He was used to his mom acting this way since Kyle had died, but his new friend shouldn’t have to suffer through it. He swallowed hard, raised his head, and snuck a glance across the table. Carmen was studying the food on her plate, looking as uncomfortable as Justin felt.

"I just lost track of time," his mom went on, choking down a sob. "And I forgot. I forgot I had it in the oven . . ." She trailed off.

His dad gave her an understanding look and reached across the table to reassure her, but his mom pulled her hand away and shook her head.

Carmen looked up and met Justin's eyes. She shot him a worried look.

"Are you having fun yet?" Justin mouthed to her. She shook her head at him as if to say *show some respect*. She sat up straighter in her chair and took a bite of her food.

"This is delicious, Mrs. Wincott," Carmen said with a smile.

"Oh," his mom said, sounding surprised—and grateful for the shift in conversation. She dabbed at her eyes with her napkin. "Thank you." She put her hands in her lap, collecting herself. Justin realized that Carmen wasn't just good with dogs, she was an expert with people, too. His mom smiled at Carmen. "We lost our oldest son recently," she said apologetically.

"Yes, ma'am. I heard. I'm sorry."

"So, Carmen," Justin's mom said, trying to change the subject. "How do you know so much about dogs?"

"My old m—my *father* used to raise pit bulls, and my brother trains them." There was a note of pride in Carmen's voice.

Justin's dad leaned toward Carmen. "You know dogfighting is illegal in Texas," he said.

Carmen's eyes got big with shock. Justin and his mom held their breath. His dad could be hard on Justin, but he was usually polite to guests. There was a note of challenge in his voice that Justin hadn't ever heard before. Then again, Justin had never brought a girl home for dinner. So there was that.

"My brother *rescues* dogs," Carmen said evenly to Raymond. "People get pit bulls when they're little and cute. Then the pits get big and people don't want them anymore, but no one will adopt them. So their owners just put them out on the street. My brother takes them in, trains them, and adopts them out."

Justin turned away so his dad wouldn't see him smile. Carmen had totally owned him. She kicked Justin under the table.

"Carmen spent the afternoon showing Justin how to work with Max," his mom added. "You should see how well Max is—" Before she could finish, Max started barking ferociously in the backyard, as if on cue.

"Is that right?" his dad said sarcastically.

Justin's heart sank. Max hadn't done his crazy barking all day. He had been perfect—but his dad hadn't been around to see it. Justin's mom looked so disappointed. They both knew that if his dad didn't come around to trusting Max, the dog was a goner. After making such great progress that day, it looked as if they were back to square one.

Then the doorbell rang.

Everyone exchanged glances across the table, until finally his mom laughed. Max had been barking for a reason—he had heard someone approaching the house before they did and wanted to warn his new pack. Justin's mom shot his dad an "I told you so" look, and Justin and Carmen grinned and exchanged a look of relief across the table. The doorbell rang again, and Justin hopped up to get it. He was glad to have an excuse to get away.

Justin swung open the door. The sound of the evening cicadas washed over him as he took in the familiar, if unexpected, figure in the doorway: Tyler Harne, his brother's best friend. Justin was so shocked he couldn't speak. Wasn't Tyler still in Afghanistan? Tyler's hair was cut short, military style, but he wore regular clothes—jeans and a collared shirt. He carried a bouquet of flowers, wilting in the evening heat.

"Look at you," Tyler said quietly, flashing his teeth. "Same little slacker I remember, only with a few more zits now." Justin just stared at him. The last time he'd seen Tyler, he was with Kyle, on the other end of a video connection from thousands of miles away. In fact, every time he'd seen Tyler, Kyle was right there by his side. The two had been inseparable since they were kids. Now Tyler was here, on their stoop, alone.

"You gonna let me in, champ?" Tyler asked, his smile tight.

Justin stepped aside without a word. Tyler moved past him into the house, where his mom and dad looked at Tyler with stunned expressions on their faces. His mom's eyes filled with tears, and her hand shot up to cover her mouth.

"I hope it's okay that I came by like this," Tyler said. "I've been home for a couple of days now, and . . ." He trailed off and held the flowers out to Justin's mom.

"Tyler," she said, stretching out her arms for a hug. "It's so good to see you."

Tyler hugged her back.

"Mrs. W., I wanted to tell you how sorry I am about—"

"Oh, hush," Justin's mom said into his shoulder. "I know. Let's not talk about that now. We've had enough waterworks here today."

She happily looked him up and down, as if to make sure he was really there.

"Didn't expect to see you back so soon," Justin's dad said, limping forward and squeezing Tyler's hand in a firm shake.

"Medical discharge, sir. I took shrapnel all up and down my back and got a few pieces lodged in my spine." He looked down at the carpet, then back up at Justin's dad. "Guess I'll be carrying these little souvenirs around for the rest of my life."

Something about the way Tyler spoke to his dad rubbed Justin the wrong way, but his mom looked so excited to see him that he pushed the feeling aside.

Justin had never really been that crazy about Tyler, even though he'd practically grown up with him. Tyler had spent more time at Kyle and Justin's house than he had at his own. He was just always . . . around.

Justin's parents loved Tyler, but Justin had never

quite trusted him. Tyler had always been the kind of kid who acted one way when someone's parents were in the room, and another when the door shut behind them. He was extra polite when Justin's mom or dad was around, telling them that he and Kyle had done their homework and that they would help Justin with his. But Tyler never so much as explained a single math problem to Justin—instead, when it was just the boys, he would try to mess with him. Tyler would make fun of Justin—calling him a serious loser or computer nerd.

The worst part was that Kyle would laugh and punch Tyler on the shoulder to tell him to lay off Justin, but if Kyle left the room, Tyler would keep on giving Justin a hard time.

Right now, though, that was the last thing Justin's parents cared about. What did it matter anymore anyway? Without Kyle here, Tyler wouldn't really be a part of their lives.

"Well," Justin's dad said to Tyler, "aren't we just a couple of beat-up old Marines."

Tyler nodded, his face serious. "Yes, sir, Mr. Wincott. Proud to stand alongside you."

"You came back just in time for the Fourth of July parade," his dad said. "I'd be proud to have you march alongside me, too."

Justin resisted the urge to roll his eyes.

"Oh, no, sir." Tyler held his hands out in front of him. "You know me. That's not my scene."

"You'll be right there with me, Tyler," Justin's dad said in a firm voice. "Marching by my side." His dad broke into a smile. "Do I make myself clear, Marine?"

"Yes, sir." Tyler raised his hand in a salute. Justin couldn't help it—he actually rolled his eyes this time.

"Does it hurt?"

Justin was surprised by the sound of Carmen's voice. She was still sitting at the table, watching the reunion. Tyler studied Carmen for a moment.

"All that metal in your back," Carmen finished.

"Yeah, it hurts," Tyler said. "But they got me on so many painkillers, I hardly notice it." He eyed Carmen carefully. "And you are?"

"This is Carmen," his mom said. "Justin's friend. She's been helping him with—" She stopped midsentence, as if something had just occurred to her. "Tyler," she said with a knowing look, "there's someone else here I think you should say hello to."

Tyler tipped his head to the side, confused. "Who's that?"

"Justin, do you want to show him?" his mom asked. Justin shrugged and stepped toward the back door.

Tyler and the others followed him. The group stepped into the darkness, and Justin heard Max's chain jangle as the dog stood up and crossed toward them. Justin's eyes adjusted to the dark, and he saw Max straining against his collar and sniffing at the air. Suddenly, he lurched forward, his eyes bulging out of his head and his ears tucked back. He started growling and barking ferociously, baring his teeth. The fur on his back stood up, and he dug at the grass with his paws.

Justin gave Carmen a worried look. She shrugged in confusion.

"Max, huh?" Tyler said, shaking his head. He had a strange expression on his face that Justin couldn't quite identify. "I heard they were gonna—you know, put him down," Tyler went on. He looked at Justin's parents. "Well, he's alive, I see."

Max strained even harder against his collar, practically choking himself. Justin's mom looked at her son with a concerned expression. He shook his head helplessly. Max had made such great progress earlier—Justin hadn't expected this. Why would Max hate Tyler? He *knew* Tyler.

"Hey, boy," Tyler said nervously to Max. "There's no *hajis* around here. You don't have to get so worked up. We're back in Texas now."

Max just flipped out harder at the sound of Tyler's voice—his barking had taken on a mad, frenzied tone. Justin was worried that he was about to get loose from his chain. Suddenly, with a huge tug, Max bolted forward and pulled the stake right out of the ground.

His eyes glowing with rage, Max lunged at Tyler, ready to rip Tyler's throat out. Tyler barely had time to take a step backward and cover his face with his hands.

Before he even knew what he was doing, Justin threw himself in Max's path.

"Stay!" Justin screamed. Max skidded to a stop but kept his eyes on Tyler and let out a low, angry growl. He crouched down, as if he were going to leap at Tyler again. Carmen reached out and grabbed Max by his choke collar.

"Stay, Max! Stay!" she commanded. Justin stood close to her and grasped Max's collar, too. Together, they managed to subdue him.

Tyler raised his hands in the air, shaking off the encounter. Justin's mom held both hands over her mouth. His dad threw open the back door.

"Let's go inside, Pam," Justin's dad said sternly. Without a word, his mom grabbed Tyler by the arm and led him inside. As Tyler took one look over his shoulder at Max, Justin saw something surprising in Tyler's eyes. He would have expected Tyler to look afraid—or maybe relieved—but instead he just looked . . . something else. For a second, Justin couldn't name it exactly, but then he realized what it was: Tyler looked angry.

TEN

THE COOL MORNING AIR HIT JUSTIN STRAIGHT IN THE face as he sped down his driveway. The gears on his bike clicked as he pedaled through his quiet neighborhood. It was still early, and he felt as if he had the whole town to himself.

He'd ridden this route a million times, always alone. Today, though, he had some company. Justin looked down at the top of Max's head as the dog trotted along beside him. Justin still had no idea why Max had freaked out on Tyler last night, but the dog—*his* dog—seemed completely fine today. In fact, Max seemed so happy when he was running—like he didn't have a care in the world.

Justin gripped the handlebars with one hand and held Max's leash in the other. Max kept pace with Justin's bike so easily that he wasn't even panting. Soon they reached the edge of the neighborhood, where the houses stopped and the woods began.

Suddenly, a man walking a giant white and black dog, a Newfoundland, came around the corner. The other dog tensed up and began barking nastily. Max's ears went forward, and a soft rumble emanated from his throat. Justin was worried—would Max flip out again, like he had at Tyler? He didn't know if he'd be able to control him without Carmen here to help. Justin came to a stop, tugged firmly on Max's collar and said, "Max, *settle*," in a firm voice, just like Carmen had taught him to do.

Max stopped growling on command. His body relaxed. He looked up at Justin expectantly, waiting for his next order. It was like the dog across the street didn't exist anymore. Justin broke into a huge grin—surprised and proud that Max had listened to him out in the world, and not just within the safe confines of their backyard.

"Attaboy, Max." They waited for the hostile Newfoundland to turn the corner. Justin studied

Max's serious brown eyes for a moment, and a thought dawned on him—this was a dog who was trained to fight dangerous enemies in a real war. Running down a paved road in small-town Texas had to be pretty boring for him, sort of like playing a too-easy level in a video game was for Justin. Maybe it was time to raise the stakes.

"You're bored, huh," Justin said to Max, who just looked at him mutely, his eyes eager. "You ready to show me what you got?"

At the sound of Justin's voice, Max cocked his head to the side and waited.

"Sit."

Max sat. Hesitantly, Justin leaned down and unhooked the leash from his collar. If Max ran off or didn't listen, Justin would be in huge trouble with his dad. But the chance that this could be awesome was worth it.

"Stay." Max stayed. "Listen, Max. You mess up now, you're grounded for life, you hear me?" The dog sat perfectly still, as though he understood everything Justin had said.

Justin rolled up the leash and jammed it into his sweatshirt pocket. With a deep breath, he took off, pedaling as fast as he could and steering his bike toward the woods. He looked down to see if Max had kept up.

But his dog was gone.

A sinking feeling landed in Justin's stomach as he screeched his bike to a halt. He whipped his head around in a panic, searching for Max.

Max was sitting in the road, exactly where Justin had left him, waiting patiently for his next command. His eyes were locked on Justin. That's when Justin realized that he'd told Max to stay, so that's what Max was doing. Nothing was going to sway this dog from his duty.

Justin's chest swelled with pride. "Max, come!" he called.

Max shot toward him, crossing the distance between them in a millisecond. Together, they headed toward the forest. Justin pedaled as hard as he could, steering his bike over crunching leaves and around jagged rocks. Max ran at his side, leaping easily over roots and zigzagging through the trees. Max looked as though he was barely breaking a sweat. He just seemed happy, relaxed, and free. For the first time in weeks, Justin felt almost the same way.

Justin and Max skidded into the bike park, where

riders raced up the wooden ramp and launched themselves into the air.

"What's up, hombre?" Chuy called out, and biked up to Justin.

"Hey, Chuy," Justin gave him a grin. Max gave the smallest wag of his tail and looked up at Justin's best friend.

Chuy looked down at Max. "Hey, Max. Don't hurt me, man," he joked.

The boys watched Carmen zip up the side of the makeshift wooden ramp and make a clean jump. She rode over to them.

"Hey, Justin," she said with a smile. She shook out her hair as she took off her helmet.

"Hey, Carmen. You looked pretty cool out there."

"Thanks." Carmen hopped off her bike, eased it onto the ground, and knelt down next to Max, who sat at Justin's side. She held out her hand and let him smell her palm. "Hey, Max. We in a better mood today, pal?" Max's wet nose nudged at Carmen, as if he was looking for more carnitas. Justin could tell that Carmen really knew how to get along with dogs.

Justin was surprised at how happy he was to see her—and how normally she was treating him—especially after the weirdness of dinner and the awkwardness of sitting in the car with Justin's mom, who had driven Carmen home last night. Carmen had every reason to want nothing to do with Justin today, but instead she was being totally chill. Justin realized he was staring at her, and she was just smiling at him.

Chuy looked from Justin to Carmen and back and rolled his eyes. "Yo, Justin, I was gonna call you," Chuy said, "but I didn't want to call your house in case your dad answered. Why don't you get a cell phone and join the twenty-first century?"

"Ha. I would," Justin grumbled, "but my dad won't buy me one."

Carmen shot him a sharp look.

"Uh, I mean," Justin said with a grin, "being the fine, upstanding gentleman that he is."

Carmen punched Justin playfully on the arm. "Stop it with that sarcasm, would you? Your dad's not so bad," she said.

Max snapped to attention when Carmen hit Justin. He hopped to his feet and stepped closer to Justin, as if to protect him. Max began sniffing at Chuy, who made an exaggerated scared face and took a big step backward.

"Justin, man, you have got yourself the ultimate guard dog," Chuy said. "I heard he tore up your brother's friend last night—had his teeth all up in his throat." Chuy pretended to claw at his own neck and made it sound as if he were getting strangled. Max looked confused.

Justin cracked up, genuinely laughing for the first time since he could remember. He patted Max on the head reassuringly. Even Carmen had to smile at her cousin's antics.

"Chuy, man," Justin said. "Sometimes I wish I could be you, just so the world would be so awesome all the time."

"The world *is* awesome, dude," Chuy replied with a sideways grin. "Y'all just have a bad attitude. Crazy awesome things are happening all the time."

"Yo, Justin!" a trio of voices called out from across the clearing. It was a group of boys who were a couple of years older than Justin. They stood up on their pedals, lingering at the top of a path that led deeper into the woods. "We're hitting Cutter's Run. Come on!"

"Cool!" Justin shouted back. "Catch up with you in a minute."

"Catch up?" Carmen asked in surprise. "To those guys? On *that* trail?"

Justin shrugged, enjoying his chance to show off a little. "Why not?" he replied as he snapped on his bike helmet.

"What about Max?" she asked, sounding a bit worried.

Max stood at attention by his side. His mouth was open and his tail wagging with excitement.

"Keep up if you can, boy."

Without another word, Justin spun his bike around, shot forward onto the steepest ramp in the clearing, and executed a perfect jump, landing with hardly a sound. His shock absorbers bounced with his weight. Max sprinted close by, following Justin between two trees and down a narrow path that sloped sharply downward.

Justin glanced back to see that Carmen's eyes were wide with disbelief. Chuy took one look at her and burst out laughing. "Oh, I see. Looks like you don't know my boy Justin too well yet."

"I know your boy has problems," she replied with a shake of her head.

"Come on. Let's go see just how bad his problems

are," Chuy said as he pushed off to follow Justin. Carmen hopped on her bike and pumped her legs to catch up with Chuy, Justin, and Max.

Now that Carmen was following him, Justin sped up, ready to demonstrate his skills. He loved the moment when the trees closed in all around him. It was as though someone had pulled a shade down over the day, sealing him inside the bright green forest. Light filtered down through the trees and sounds were muted. Justin breathed in sharply through his nose, the pungent scent of wet leaves and dirt filling his nostrils. He rode hard, easily catching up to the older kids in front. Max darted along by his side, his paws barely touching the ground, his tail pointed straight upward. It was almost as if Max already knew every rock and root in the woods. He leaped and sidestepped and hopped through the rough terrain. Justin avoided the bigger boulders, and lifted his wheel over the tangled roots that crisscrossed his path. Together, they zigzagged down the steep hill.

Justin could hear the boys whooping and hollering in front of him, and Chuy gasping for air behind him. Justin and Max rounded a curve and headed down an even steeper stretch of the trail. One of the boys fell. Another swerved to the side, kicking up dirt as he braked. The third kid looked like he was about to collapse from exhaustion.

But Justin felt awesome. He raced past them all, Max by his side. They barreled downhill, picking up speed.

"Yo, Justin!" one of the boys called. "That's Cutter's Doom, man! Stop!"

Carmen and Chuy skidded to a halt by the group of boys.

"Justin, stop!" Carmen called after him.

But Justin had no intention of stopping now. He and Max headed down a particularly steep grade, then, using his downhill momentum, Justin hurtled forward up the next hill. He was pumping harder than ever. He reached the top and crested the mound. For a millisecond, he felt suspended between up and down, released from gravity, perched on top of the world. Then he tipped forward and headed downhill again, straight for the edge of a cliff—straight for the drop-off known as Cutter's Doom.

Justin and Kyle had ridden in these woods together as kids—often with Tyler by their side. When he was younger, Justin had to work twice as hard as the big boys to get here, but now he would beat them. Too bad Kyle wasn't here to see how fast and strong a rider his little brother was.

Every time they approached Cutter's Doom, Tyler would egg Kyle on, prodding him to make the jump. It was a legendary leap—about twenty feet across a ravine that must have been fifty feet deep. The only way to cross it was to approach the sharp drop-off at top speed, and to lift your front tire at the last possible second. There was no room for hesitation, no margin for error. Only one or two kids they knew had ever jumped Cutter's Doom. Kyle always waved off Tyler when he dared him to try it. Even as a kid, Justin had noticed that *Tyler* never volunteered to give it a go.

Though Justin had never said it out loud to Kyle and Tyler, he always told himself he'd make the jump one day. The last time the three of them had come out here together, not long before Kyle and Tyler enlisted, Justin swore to himself he was going to do it, right in front of them. But then his bike got a flat tire, and Tyler and Kyle had to take turns carrying Justin's bike in one hand as they steered their own bikes with the other, and Justin walked home.

Justin never felt like trying again after that. At some

point after Kyle shipped out to Afghanistan, Justin stopped even thinking about it. Yet today, for the first time in ages, Justin wanted to try it. He felt he *had* to try. Even though Kyle wasn't here to see it—and would *never* be here to see it—it felt to Justin as if he was doing it for his brother.

Justin could feel the energy coursing through his legs and into the bike. He had never felt so free. Max raced along, panting. His tongue bobbed out of his mouth.

"Chuy," one of the other kids called out, "your boy has lost his mind."

"Justin!" Carmen screamed again.

But Justin kept moving. He barreled toward the edge of the drop. Max stopped just a few inches from the cliff's edge and barked sharply at Justin.

Justin didn't stop. At the last second, he pulled up on his handlebars, not looking down at the deep abyss below. He kept his gaze on the stretch of land on the other side. Suddenly, he was flying, completely weightless as he soared across the canyon.

Max was barking somewhere behind him. The wind whipped in Justin's ears. The ground approached quickly, and suddenly his front tire slammed into the dirt, and he bounced up and down on his seat.

For the first time ever, he'd made it across Cutter's Doom.

"Waaaaaaahoooooooo!" Justin shouted, pumping a fist into the air. His chest heaved and he bent over to catch his breath. His legs and arms tingled with adrenaline.

Max was still barking on the other side of the cliff. He ran back and forth along the edge, trying to get to Justin. His voice echoed across the canyon.

"Justin, you're crazy!" Carmen called across. "Your dog has more sense than you!" Justin couldn't be sure from that distance, but he thought that maybe he saw the flicker of a smile on her face.

"*Oh, Justinnnnnn!*" Chuy mocked in a girlish voice. "*Oh, I was so scared you were going to break a nail!*" Justin laughed as Carmen punched Chuy hard on the shoulder. From the distance across the ravine, Justin could see Chuy rubbing his arm in pain.

★ ★ ★

JUSTIN ROLLED UP IN FRONT OF HIS HOUSE, HIS CHEEKS practically sore from smiling. Max trotted along by his side, barely worn out by all the activity. Justin hopped off his bike and wheeled along the side of the house. He reached the backyard, lay his bike down on the grass, and froze.

Right smack in the middle of the lawn was a giant metal dog crate. The bars were thick slats. The latch was massive and solid metal. The monstrosity glinted in the late afternoon sunlight.

Justin knew exactly who was to blame for this. He walked Max over to the crate, swung open the wide door, and urged his dog to go inside.

"Go on, boy. Get in there," Justin said gently. Max hesitated, sniffing cautiously at the floor of the crate. "It's okay, buddy. Go on."

Max stared up at him with sad eyes.

"Inside, Max." Justin couldn't look at him. He turned away until Max had slunk into the crate. Justin shut the door firmly behind him and slipped the latch into place. "Be right back with some water," he said, snatching Max's water bowl up from the ground.

Justin stomped into the house, clenching and unclenching his fists.

His dad sat at the kitchen table reading the paper.

"It's for his own good," his dad said before Justin even had a chance to speak.

Justin opened his mouth to say something nasty, but no words came out. What was the point? He knew his dad well enough to know that he wasn't going to budge on this. Justin dropped Max's bowl into the sink and filled it to the brim. He carried it to the door, purposely sloshing water onto the floor as he went.

Just before he could step back outside, his dad said, "I expect you at work after the holiday. Eight o'clock sharp."

Justin kept his back to his dad. He gritted his teeth together to stop himself from saying anything he'd regret.

"You need to start pulling your weight around here, Justin."

Justin didn't respond. He stepped through the back door and kicked it shut behind him, heading for Max's new cage.

ELEVEN

THE *RAT-A-TAT-TAT* OF DRUMS ECHOED DOWN THE town's main street, announcing the Fourth of July parade. The Lufkin High School band rounded the corner and was heading right past Justin and his mom. Behind them, a group of young girls twirled batons up into the air and caught them. The large crowd applauded and cheered—everyone in town was here to watch the celebration. Up next was a bright red fire engine. Firemen hung off the sides, clutching small American flags in their large hands. The men waved proudly at the crowd as the truck rumbled past.

Justin used to love this parade when he was a kid.

He'd sit on Kyle's shoulders—though Kyle was only a few years older, he was able to hold Justin up high enough for him to see the floats over the crowd. Now Justin was tall enough to see for himself, but he hated the parade: the false smiles, the happy patriotism of people who'd never watched their big brother leave for a war—and come home in a coffin.

Plus, the last person he felt like cheering for was his dad, who would pass by soon with the other veterans from their town. He still hadn't quite forgiven his dad for forcing Max into a cage. Justin thrust his hands deep into his jean's pockets.

Justin spotted Chuy and his family camped out directly across the street, right in front of the pharmacy. He scanned the group for Carmen. She was toward the back, holding a Chihuahua in the crook of her arm. He watched her for a moment, smiling to himself.

His mom tapped him with the back of her hand. "Here they come," she said excitedly.

Sure enough, a cluster of veterans marched in time to the music. They were men and women of all ages—some of them had to be in their eighties. They smiled and looked from one side of the street to the other. Justin spotted his dad in the center of the group. He wore a Marines cap and a red jacket. He limped along, his back upright and stiff, one hand saluting and the other waving at the crowd. Justin didn't wave back.

"Ray!" his mom called out. His dad turned at the sound of his wife's voice. He spotted her and Justin and nodded. His parents held each other's gaze for a moment, and Justin saw tears spring to his mother's eyes.

Walking right next to his dad was Tyler. He wore civilian clothes, and he looked uncomfortable marching down the middle of the street, as if he didn't like the feeling of so many eyes on him. Justin's father reached out a hand and placed it on Tyler's shoulder. Justin, who was already ticked off at his dad, was suddenly filled with a feeling so intense that it surprised even him. It was more than anger, and it wasn't just directed at his father—it was directed at the unfairness of the world.

Justin was mad beyond words that his brother was dead, but he was sad and frustrated, too. He felt helpless to make his parents feel better, to make himself feel better. Seeing Tyler marching with his dad brought all these feelings out in Justin. It was wrong that Tyler was there with his dad, instead of his brother. *It should be Kyle.*

★ ★ ★

ONCE HE REACHED THE END OF THE PARADE ROUTE, Justin's dad doubled back and met up with his wife and Justin. The last of the procession was trickling by—mostly a handful of stragglers with noisemakers. The sun had gone down, which meant the firecrackers had started up. Justin could hear them popping, the sound drifting over from parking lots and alleyways. Usually he'd be out there with Chuy, lighting them, too, but he didn't feel like it this year.

Justin and his parents settled in for the town's fireworks show. Justin leaned back against the hood of a car, while his parents stood side by side nearby. The sky darkened to black, then suddenly exploded with color and light. The loud booms started up a split second later—a symphony of crackles and blasts. Justin's eardrums tingled. He felt the deep bass of each explosion in his bones.

He looked around at the upturned faces of the crowd. Everyone else was captivated by the show. They *oohed* and *aahed* with each new burst. His mom leaned her head on his dad's shoulder. His dad took her hand and squeezed it.

Justin felt tense and jumpy. He couldn't relax—or

escape the feeling that there was something sinister about the fireworks tonight. Instead of seeming like a celebration, they seemed . . . harsh and dangerous. Justin found himself wondering if the explosions in the Lufkin summer sky sounded anything like a rocket grenade going off in Afghanistan.

That's when he realized what was bothering him: *Max*. Panic shot through Justin. He remembered what Sergeant Reyes had said—that Max was suffering from PTSD and couldn't bear the sound of loud noises. What did that mean for poor Max, who at that very moment was locked in a cage, with no way of escaping the explosions? Justin knew Max was probably flipping out, and felt horrible for leaving his dog all alone on the most traumatizing of nights.

Without a word to his parents, Justin jumped off the car and pushed his way through the crowd. He walked quickly, then jogged, then broke into a full run. The fireworks lit up the road as he ran. He raced home as fast as he could, his side cramping up as he turned onto his block. He dashed past his mom's car and down the side of the house into the backyard.

Justin stopped a few feet from Max's crate and put his hands on his knees, catching his breath. It was worse than he had thought. Max was completely crazy with fear. He spun in tight circles in his cage, whining and barking. He howled desperately with every new blast in the sky. Justin's heart leaped in his chest. He'd seen Max angry, he'd even been afraid of Max, but Justin had never seen him so scared.

How was he going to calm down Max?

"Max, it's okay," he said soothingly. "Take it easy, boy. I'm here now. It's just fireworks."

Max whimpered sadly. For a second Justin thought he had soothed him, but when a new firework lit up the night, Max barked and howled wildly. Justin had an idea—he ran over to the back door of the house and opened it. Then he ran over to Max's cage. He'd bring the dog inside.

"I'm gonna open the door, Max," he said gently. "Then you can come out, buddy." Justin swung open the door to the crate, but Max just backed away from him. "Come on, Max," Justin begged. "Come on out, please. It's okay."

Max spun in circles, all his hair standing on edge and his tail between his legs. "Let's go inside the house," Justin said. "Come on, Max, let's go."

Justin took a step toward the house to demonstrate

what he meant. Max suddenly stopped twirling and snarled at Justin. Justin froze—this was not going well at all. Had Max became dangerous again? His dog glared at him from inside the open crate.

Another shower of light and sound burst down from above. Max pressed himself into the back corner of his cage, howling and barking. His tail hung even lower between his legs. Justin sighed. He knew he didn't have any other choice if he wanted to help Max. He stepped toward the crate. He wished there was another way, but he knew there wasn't.

"Easy, Max. Easy. Listen—I'm coming in, okay?"

Max let out a little snort, but stayed pressed against the bars, his head down, his scared eyes looking up at Justin.

Justin held up his hands in a surrender gesture. He spoke softly as he bent over and stepped into the cage, which wasn't tall enough for him to stand up in. "Here I come, buddy. It's okay, pal."

Justin paused, then little by little crept farther toward Max.

"Good boy, Max. I'm here. It's just fireworks." Justin slipped down to the ground next to Max and pulled his knees in, cross-legged. Max sniffed at him. Slowly, carefully, Justin reached out and put his hand on Max's neck. Max stayed put. Justin caressed his fur. "It's okay, boy. You're okay."

Max's frantic breathing slowed down. He lowered his head and pressed it against Justin's chest. Justin hooked his arm around Max's neck and scratched behind his ears. Max lay down, resting his head completely in Justin's lap. Justin pulled him closer until Max's entire body was on his lap. They'd never been this close before, and Max's fur felt soft and warm. Justin felt some knot inside of his chest uncoil, like his own pain and grief over Kyle was falling away from him. The two of them huddled together, their breath falling into the same rhythm, as the fireworks lit up the night sky in a bright burst of gold.

TWELVE

THE NEXT MORNING CAME WAY TOO SOON, AND THE last place Justin wanted to be was at his dad's business, Open Range Storage. He let out a giant yawn and scrunched up his eyes. Eight a.m. was way too early for a summer morning—especially because he'd had to take Max for a walk before work.

Justin desperately wanted to put on his headphones, but his dad had told him it was "unprofessional." Like there was anyone around to notice. Justin had gotten up at the crack of dawn to come down to the storage facility and sit in front of a table fan in the office. He listened to his own stomach grumble and realized he might actually prefer to be in math class.

As if the day hadn't been annoying enough, suddenly Tyler showed up. Apparently his dad had offered the guy a job. Considering that the phone hadn't rung once in several hours, Justin wasn't sure what there was for him to do. But if there was only enough work for one of them, Justin hoped his dad would choose Tyler.

As his dad showed Tyler around the outdoor facility, Justin eavesdropped through the open window.

"We've got twenty-five eight-by-ten storage spaces on this side," his dad explained. "And twenty six-by-twelves on the other side. Right now, we're at about half capacity." Justin's father sighed. "Hard times."

Justin heard the rattling crash of a metal gate coming down. "Nowadays," his dad went on, "most people would rather let things go than spend money holding on to them. Anyone who leaves his stuff here for more than three months without paying relinquishes his right to his property. I keep what I can use and sell off the rest." Justin heard the rumble of a gate going up. "This one here is getting cleaned out tomorrow. Feel free to grab anything you want."

"Yes, sir. Thanks, Mr. Wincott," Tyler said. He spoke like he was really extra polite, but Justin thought he just sounded fake.

"Name's Ray, son. 'Mr. Wincott' is some guy you knew when you were a kid."

"Yes, sir—Mist—Ray."

Justin pretend-gagged alone in the office. He imagined Tyler dropping to his knees and bowing down to his dad.

"Your shift will be from six to six," Justin's dad said as he and Tyler came back into the office together. Neither man looked in his direction. "We don't have a security guard." He tapped the gun in the holster on his hip. "We don't really need one." His dad stepped over to the supply closet and pulled out a dark green zippered jumpsuit with the Open Range logo over the front pocket. "It's not much compared to the uniform you're used to."

Tyler took the outfit from him and smiled widely. "I'll be proud to wear it."

Now Justin really wanted to barf.

"Tyler," his dad said, "the truth is, there isn't much to this job, especially for a young man with your skills. You'll be bored out of your mind here."

"Excitement is about the last thing I need," Tyler said. "A little boredom suits me just fine right now. It's why I came to you about the job in the first place. No offense intended, of course."

“None taken,” Justin’s dad replied. Justin grimaced—if he had said what Tyler had just said, his dad would have grounded him for a week.

Justin was surprised to see his dad limp over to the mini-fridge under his desk and take out two beers. It was early for him to start drinking. He handed one to Tyler, who shook his head. “Thank you, but it doesn’t mix with my meds, sir. I mean . . . Ray.”

Justin saw his dad shrug and put one can back. He cracked open the other beer and took a long sip. “I heard your old man is up in Tucson these days.”

“Yup. He just finished a stint at State,” Tyler replied.

“Sorry to hear it.”

“Three squares a day. Prison works for some,” Tyler said with a tight smile. Justin remembered when Tyler’s dad was arrested. He was only a kid when it happened, but even then he could sense that it was really tough on Tyler and his mom. Kyle had told Justin it was part of why Tyler decided to join the military in the first place—to get as far away from his family as possible. Justin couldn’t help but wonder why, after all that, Tyler had wanted to come back to Texas.

Justin’s dad studied Tyler for a moment. “If you need somewhere to stay, son, we’ve got the old spare room we can make up for you.”

The spare room? *That* was Kyle's room! Justin hated the thought of Tyler living in his house, with his parents fawning over him the way they used to coo at Kyle. As if Kyle could be replaced.

"I'm crashing with some buddies," Tyler said, to Justin's relief. "You've already given me more than I deserve. I just wish there was something I could do for you in return."

"Well," his dad said, taking another swig of beer, as if for courage. "There is one thing."

Justin couldn't help but stare at his dad from the other side of the room. What could Tyler possibly do for him? His dad tilted his head in Justin's direction, indicating that he didn't want his son to hear what he was going to say. "Let's step outside, shall we?" he said to Tyler.

"Sure, sir." Tyler followed him out the door to a shady spot between two storage units—right by the open window. Justin could still hear them as clearly as if they were in the room.

"You were there," his dad said in a low, serious voice.

"There, sir?" Tyler asked, confused.

"When my boy . . ." He trailed off. Tyler was silent. Justin's stomach did a queasy flip. "I need to know, Tyler."

"Know what?" Tyler asked quietly.

"How my boy died."

"Sir, Kyle was the best friend I ever had, and the bravest Marine I—"

"Tyler," Justin's dad cut him off. "I need to know." His voice was firm but pleading.

Tyler paused, then spoke in one long stream of words. Justin wished he could see his face.

"We were out on that last patrol, looking for a *haji* arms cache, when it hit the fan. Rocket-propelled grenades going off, bullets flying, you name it. It was like hell on earth." Tyler paused again. "Then, well, sir . . . the dog lost it."

"The *dog*?"

Justin sucked in his breath. He couldn't believe what he was hearing.

"Yes, sir," Tyler continued. "And you know Kyle. He tried to keep the dog calm when he should have been finding cover. Then it went for him and made him lose control of his weapon." Tyler was silent for a long moment. Justin held his breath, unsure if he wanted Tyler to continue. "The next thing I knew, Kyle was hit."

There was complete quiet from outside. Justin was afraid to move, for fear he'd miss anything.

"The dog came at me next," Tyler said. "I was about to put him down, when some of the other guys came up and stopped me. They didn't see what happened, so they prevented me from doing what I should have done." Tyler's voice cracked. "I am so sorry, Ray."

"You did what you could," Justin's dad said so quietly Justin could barely hear him.

"Yes, sir. Thank you, sir."

"Now if you don't mind, I'd like to be alone now." His dad's voice was shaky.

"Of course, sir."

Justin heard Tyler's footsteps fade away, then his truck start up in the distance. Justin sat by himself inside the office, his head spinning. It was hard to learn about Kyle's last minutes—just hearing the words said out loud made his chest start to hurt again, like it had in the days right after Kyle died. But there was something else, too—something that didn't feel right. Something in Tyler's voice, maybe. Or in the story he'd told. The hair on the back of Justin's neck stood up when he replayed Tyler's words: ". . . *it went for him and made him lose control of his weapon . . .*"

That just didn't sound like Max.

The door flew open and banged against the wall.

His dad stood in the doorway, his hands balled into fists at his sides. His jaw was set and his eyes were filled with rage. Justin understood the look on his father's face, and he knew exactly what his dad planned to do.

"Justin, stay here and watch the place."

Before Justin could stop his father, he'd snatched his keys up off his desk and stormed out of the office, his hand on his holster. Justin wasn't going to let him do this . . . he followed his dad and jumped on his bike. He heard his dad's SUV start up, then screech out of the lot.

Justin zipped through the automatic gate just as it was closing behind the SUV. He pedaled as hard as he could, hoping he could make it home in time to stop his dad. In time to save Max.

THIRTEEN

JUSTIN FELT LIKE HIS LUNGS WERE BURSTING THROUGH his chest. He'd never ridden this hard for this long, but he couldn't slow down. He had to get home in time—before his dad really went off the deep end and did something he'd regret.

Justin knew that his dad was still grieving over Kyle's death, and that it was painful for him to see Tyler alive and well instead of his own son. Max was the last connection his dad had to Kyle—and the possibility that Max had caused Kyle's death, even indirectly, was too much for his father to bear.

His dad had snapped.

Justin also knew with more certainty than he'd ever known anything in his life, that he wasn't going to let anything bad happen to Max. Even if that meant getting between his dog and his own father.

He pulled up to his house, threw his bike down on the front lawn, and raced into the backyard. His father was standing in front of Max's crate, his gun drawn and pointed at Max's head. The gate was open, but Max pressed himself against the back bars.

"Let's go, Max," his dad seethed. "Get in the car."

His mom stood a few feet away, the door hanging open behind her.

"Ray, please," she pleaded. "What are you doing? Stop!"

"Dad, don't—" Justin joined in. He looked at Max as he spoke. Max didn't take his eyes off Justin's father.

"*Now*, Max," Justin's dad said, his voice louder.

Max stayed put. His tail sank down between his hind legs. Justin's dad stepped forward and leaned over, reaching an arm into the cage. He grabbed at Max's collar, but Max lowered himself into an attack stance and growled—long and low and mean. His dad snapped his hand back.

"Don't make me do this here," Justin's dad said in

a voice so quiet and cold it sent chills down Justin's spine. His dad cocked the safety on the gun.

"Dad—"

"Ray—"

Justin's father continued to ignore his wife and son. He only saw Max.

"You're not going to hurt anyone else in this family."

"Ray! What are you talking about?" Justin's mom was starting to get angry at her husband.

"This animal killed our son."

"What? What are you saying? Max would never do that, Ray." Tears streamed down his mom's face.

"She's right, Dad. I heard what Tyler said. But Max wouldn't do that. Not to Kyle."

"You don't know anything about this dog," his dad spat.

All of a sudden, it was clear to Justin how to get through to his dad.

"But I knew Kyle," Justin said. He stepped around his dad and stood between the gun and the cage.

"No—Justin—" his mom cried out.

Justin ignored her.

"Justin, get out of my way."

"Dad, listen to me. Kyle would never have put his

buddies' lives on the line by heading straight into a dangerous situation with a dog he couldn't trust. You know that as well as I do."

His dad seemed to take in Justin's words. He dropped the gun to his side and glared at his son, but it wasn't the usual disdainful look that Justin had come to expect. Justin saw something in his dad's expression he'd never seen before: a grudging respect. It was almost as if he was impressed that Justin had stood up to him.

Justin's dad thought for a long moment before speaking. "One time," he said, his tone steely. "That dog messes up *one time* and he's going back to Maitland. That's the last word on it." He stormed into the house.

Justin and his mom stood mutely on the lawn. Max relaxed and dropped to the floor of his cage. He put his head down on his front paws and half closed his eyes. Justin reached in and scratched him behind the ears. Max nosed at his hand, then put his head back down. Justin pulled back, swung the heavy metal door shut, and clicked the latch into place. He didn't know if he was trying to keep Max in or his dad out.

Justin's head was spinning with a million questions about what Tyler had said today, but he knew who might have some answers. There was only one person who understood Max as well as Kyle had—and who could help Justin get to the bottom of what had really happened with Kyle and Max in Afghanistan.

★ ★ ★

JUSTIN RODE ALL THE WAY TO MAITLAND ON HIS BIKE. IT was far, but he barely noticed—he was too determined to get there to talk to Sergeant Reyes.

Justin hadn't even bothered to call ahead. He showed up at the kennel and stood awkwardly in front of the receptionist, who eyed him suspiciously. He was sure he looked pretty weird—a sweaty, stressed-out kid showing up without an appointment. Luckily, though, Reyes was in the office and, after the receptionist called him from the front desk, was available to meet with him right away.

Justin waited for him in the lobby. When Reyes came to get him, just the sight of the tall soldier, with his upright bearing and confident gait, made Justin feel better.

"Hi, Sergeant Reyes," Justin said, suddenly embarrassed to be there. "I don't know if you remember me."

"Of course I remember you, Justin." Reyes crushed Justin's hand in a firm shake. Justin tried not to wince at the pain. Reyes led Justin down a long hallway to his office. They sat down on opposite sides of his desk. "It's good to see you again. How are your folks?"

"All right, I guess, sir."

"And how's Max?"

Justin swallowed hard. "Well, sir, that's actually what I wanted to talk to you about." He hesitated for a moment, trying to figure out how to ask what he needed to know. "Was Max a bad dog?"

Reyes studied Justin carefully but kindly. "Max was as good a dog as any that has passed through this facility. Why?"

"Could he have ever hurt Kyle?" Justin felt horrible the moment the words came out of his mouth.

"Dogs can bite their handlers. It happens." Reyes leaned forward in his chair. "But I don't think that's what you're asking me, Justin."

Justin forced himself to utter the words he'd been afraid to speak out loud. "Could he ever have turned on Kyle in the middle of a battle?"

There. He'd said it.

Reyes looked concerned. "What would make you think something like that?"

Justin dropped his gaze down to the floor. "My

brother's friend Tyler—I guess he was with him when he died. And he told my dad some things about . . . about Max."

Sergeant Reyes turned to the computer on his desk and tapped a few things into the keyboard.

"Tyler . . . Tyler Harne?"

Justin nodded. Just hearing Tyler's full name created a pit in his stomach.

"Did Harne tell your dad why he's back home five months early?"

There was something in Reyes's tone that struck Justin as odd. Was he implying that Tyler had come home for some unusual reason? That meant Tyler had lied about why he was back.

"I guess he got injured or something," Justin replied.

"Or something," Reyes said grimly. "'Administrative separation.' I don't see anything here about an injury."

Justin thought back to the night Tyler stood in his living room, telling his family and Carmen that he had shrapnel in his spine. He remembered Carmen asking Tyler if it hurt. Had she sensed something fishy about Tyler's story even then?

"So are you saying he lied to us?" Justin asked. So many thoughts competed for attention in his mind. If

Tyler hadn't told the truth about why he'd come home, then why wouldn't he lie about Max? It seemed as though Tyler was trying to cover up something big . . . but what could be worth going to so much trouble?

Whatever it was, Justin was determined to figure it out. He had a feeling that Tyler was trying to keep something hidden, and it had to do with Kyle and Max. If he could figure out Tyler's secret, maybe he could save his dog's life . . . even if it was too late to save Kyle's.

Reyes opened his mouth to speak, then seemed to think better of it and snapped it shut. Then he opened it again and said, "That's all the information I can get here. But I'll look into it." He stood up from his chair and thumbed through a neat stack of DVDs on a bookshelf. "In the meantime . . ." He handed a disc in its case to Justin. "This is classified, so don't get me in trouble, okay?"

Justin took the disc with a shaky hand and nodded. He had no idea what Reyes was giving him, but if it was classified, it had to be important. Did it have anything to do with whatever Tyler was up to—or would it tell him more about Max's behavior? It had been a day of surprises and revelations—why not one more?

“For your eyes only,” Reyes said firmly.

Justin looked down at the label on the case. There were two words written in neat capital letters: WINCOTT/MAX.

FOURTEEN

THE DVD IN JUSTIN'S SWEATSHIRT POCKET BUMPED against his leg as he pedaled over to Chuy's house. He had gone home to get Max, who trotted along at his side. He'd promised his mom that they were just going for a short walk.

They pulled into Chuy's yard to the sound of a thousand Chihuahuas yipping from inside the house. Max's already pointy ears stood up even taller. He looked over at Justin as if to say *what are you getting me into?*

Justin grinned at Max. "Don't worry, Max. They're going to love you."

Max sniffed at the lawn and followed his nose toward the front door. They headed inside.

"What's up, J.?" Chuy said from the couch.

"Hi, Justin," Carmen said, a big grin on her face. She looked happy to see him, but Justin was pretty sure that he was happier to see her. Just looking at her made his stomach do a little dance. "Hey, Max," she said, leaning down to pat the dog. Max wagged his tail and let out a sweet whimper. He was happy to see Carmen, too.

"Oh," Chuy said nervously when Max made noise. Chuy scooted up onto the back of the couch to put some distance between himself and Max. "Hello, Max."

Justin ignored his friend and held out the disc to Carmen.

"So, what is this thing?" Carmen asked, reaching for it.

"I have no idea, but apparently it's top secret," he said, holding it up. "I'm not supposed to show it to anyone else. But I'm making an exception for you guys."

Carmen kept her hand out. "All right," she said, "then hand it over."

Justin dropped it into her palm. She walked over to the television and slid the disc into the DVD player.

"Check this out!" Chuy shouted from behind them.

Justin and Carmen spun around to see Chuy pointing at Max where he lay on the ground. He was covered from head to toe in squirming, wagging, wiggling, sniffing Chihuahuas. They climbed all over him, nudging their noses into his fur. Max held his head up high, trying to remain as dignified as possible. They all burst out laughing. "Look at the little guys!" Chuy cackled. "They think they can take down a giant war dog!"

"Show them how it's done, Max," Justin said as Chuy bent down and encouraged the tiny dogs to climb Max.

Justin and Carmen stood together in front of the television. Chuy sat behind them on the couch.

"It's got my brother and Max's names on it," Justin said as the DVD started up. "It's some kind of military dog training instructions, maybe?"

"So it's top secret?" Chuy asked. "I'm gonna tell Al Qaeda the army feeds our dogs Kibbles 'n Bits. It'll be the end of America."

Carmen ignored Chuy and looked at Justin. "So you haven't watched it yet?" she asked.

He shook his head and looked at his two friends. "I thought I'd wait to watch it with someone who could make heads or tails of it."

"Very punny," Chuy said. "Very, very punny of you, Justin."

Justin laughed, and Max's ears perked up at the sound of his voice.

"Justin," Carmen said, studying Max, "there's no big secret to this. Max just has to know you want him. And there's no faking it." She took a step closer to Justin. "Or are you one of those guys who just uses his dog to pick up girls?" She stood so close to him, she had to tilt her head back to look him in the eye. Justin swallowed hard. He hoped Carmen couldn't see the beads of sweat breaking out on his forehead.

"*Squeeeeeeeaaaaaaak!*"

They both jumped at the sound of Chuy's voice. He had snuck up right behind them.

"You hear that?" Chuy asked. Justin couldn't decide if he was mad at Chuy for interrupting—or grateful. "That's the sound of the third wheel squeaking, people. Come on—this is *my* house!"

Carmen crossed her arms and glared at him. "Sorry to interrupt your important activities. Like hiding in your room and spending the entire day on Instagram."

Chuy threw up his hands in frustration and headed for the back door. "You guys are making me throw up a little in my mouth. I'm going outside," he said, letting the screen door slam behind him. Justin wasn't sure if Chuy was just acting overly dramatic, or if he actually felt left out. It wasn't like Chuy to walk away from some "top secret" information. He would have to smooth things over with his friend—after he watched the video with Carmen.

Justin shrugged and turned back to Carmen, realizing that he was standing closer to her than ever, practically nose to nose. He gulped.

Carmen held his gaze for a second. "Let's watch it," she finally said.

"Okay," he replied, his voice a little unsteady.

They sat next to each other on the couch. Justin pressed Play on the remote and the black screen suddenly filled with light.

The video showed a tiny, fuzzy lump of a puppy rolling around on the grass. His fur was downy and pale, and his paws were way too big for his body. Justin recognized his curious brown eyes immediately.

They heard a man's voice off camera. "Hi, Max!" the voice said. "Hi, buddy. Hi, little guy." A large hand appeared in the frame, rubbing Max's soft tummy as he rolled around on his back. Justin couldn't help but smile as he looked at puppy-Max.

The scene changed, and a slightly larger Max, now

in full control of his limbs, raced after a ball. He was little but fast. He snatched up the ball in his mouth and zoomed back toward the camera. He dropped it at the feet of whoever was filming and looked up into the lens with a dog's version of a smile. His mouth hung open, his pink tongue dangling to the side.

The video cut to a midsized Max, his fur darker. He had finally grown into his giant paws. He ran up a ramp and down the other side, then zigzagged through a slalom set up in the dirt. He leaped over bars set at different heights. He moved smoothly, effortlessly. *That explained how Max was able to run through the woods so easily,* Justin thought.

In the next scene, Max was fully grown, a regal animal with his ears pointed straight up to the sky. His long legs and tapered snout only made him seem more graceful. He sat at attention, watching someone off camera.

"Good boy, Max. Stay."

A dull, throbbing ache radiated through Justin's chest. He knew that voice. *It was Kyle's.*

A shadow moved across the camera, and there he was—Kyle, squatting down in front of Max and grabbing him right behind the ears. Max sniffed at Kyle's face, then began licking his cheeks and nose.

"Attaboy, Max!" Kyle laughed. He squeezed his eyes shut and grimaced a little at all the slobber, but Justin could tell he loved it. Max's tail thumped against the ground.

The film cut to Kyle standing near the camera, while Max sat on a dirt road a few feet ahead of him. Max looked at Kyle, his body relaxed but poised for action. His eyes were full of anticipation as he waited for Kyle's command. The camera rolled, but Kyle said nothing for a few seconds. He was making Max wait.

"Max, *go search*," he said finally. Max hopped up and bolted off down the road. He stopped, sniffed, and skittered across the dirt to let Kyle know he had found something. "Good job, Max!" Kyle called out. Justin had never seen Max actually doing his job—or Kyle for that matter. He knew Max was insanely strong and fast and smart—but Justin now realized that his dog was more than all that: He was special. Max was the best at what he did—and Kyle had been, too.

Reyes stepped into the frame and clapped Kyle on the back. "Nice job, Marine."

"Yes, sir. Thank you, sir." Kyle was beaming. "Max, come!"

Max ran back toward Kyle and jumped up on him with his front paws.

Justin swallowed hard. There was a hot pressure behind his eyelids.

"Is that your—" Carmen asked. She looked concerned for Justin.

"Yeah."

"I can go out back if you want to be—"

"No, it's okay, you can stay." Justin paused. His mouth felt dry. "Please stay."

Justin focused his attention back on the TV as a new clip began. It looked like it was in the same training grounds as before—which Justin realized was Maitland, where they had picked up Max, and where he had met with Sergeant Reyes. A man in a full-body bite suit ran away from the camera. Max sprinted after him at top speed, his body a flash of movement. Kyle appeared at the edge of the frame.

"Max, *ATTACK*!" Kyle yelled. Max leaped on the man's back with a ferocity that made Justin suck in his breath. Max knocked the man to the ground and stood on top of him, growling. "Stop, Max," Kyle ordered. Max instantly hopped off the man and sat down by his side, totally still. He waited for Kyle's next command.

Next, a soldier in full gear pointed a plastic pistol. Max flew through the air at him, landing with full force against his chest and knocking the man to the ground. Max pinned him down with his full weight, snarling into his face.

"Max," Kyle's voice rang out off camera. "Stop." Max stopped. "Sit." Max sat. "Down!" Max lay down. Kyle stepped into the frame. He knelt down by Max and lovingly wrapped his arms around the dog's neck. Kyle looked right into the camera, gave a double thumbs-up, and flashed one of his famous grins.

The screen went black.

Justin saw himself reflected in the glass of the television. Tears streamed down his face. It was as if the full weight of missing his brother came down on him at once. He missed Kyle so much, it felt like he'd never stop missing him.

As if he sensed what Justin was feeling, Max popped up from the rug and leaned against Justin's leg. With a gentle, sweet nuzzle, he stretched his nose forward and licked the tears from Justin's cheeks. Justin put a hand around Max's neck and scratched him under the chin. They looked at each other while Carmen watched them both. He felt closer to Max than ever, and, in a funny way, closer to his brother. He finally understood what Kyle and Max meant to each other.

He also understood something else—very clearly.

Justin felt the lump in his throat go down. He could speak again.

"I knew it," Justin said.

Carmen gave him a confused look. "Knew what?"

"Tyler's a liar."

FIFTEEN

THE BACK SCREEN DOOR FLEW OPEN.

Justin's and Carmen's heads shot up to see Chuy standing in the doorway. There was a weird expression on his face—was he nervous? Something was definitely wrong.

"Justin," Chuy said, his voice a little shaky, "you better come outside."

Justin and Carmen looked at each other, eyebrows raised. Carmen shrugged. Max, sensing their unease, perked up. Justin and Carmen followed Chuy outside, Max trailing closely behind them.

As soon as Justin stepped into the yard, he frowned

and shook his head in disbelief. Chuy's gangster cousin, Emilio, leaned against his truck, arms crossed over his chest, a steely glint in his eye. He slowly looked Justin up and down. Justin tried not to let it show how angry he was that Chuy had totally set him up.

"Well, well," Emilio said, "I was just making the rounds, and look who turned up at my cousin's house." He flashed a cold smile, and his buzzed head glinted in the sunlight. "Never would have found your brother in *this* neighborhood."

Justin kept his eyes on Emilio but didn't say anything. He realized that he should have expected this—he'd asked Emilio to pay extra for the last game he'd bootlegged and Emilio wasn't the kind of guy who accepted a price hike without a fight—a gangster wasn't going to fork over two hundred dollars just because Justin said so.

"I was sorry to hear about Kyle," Emilio went on, but it was obvious that he didn't mean it—he was just trying to get under Justin's skin. The sound of his brother's name in this guy's mouth made Justin want to scream. Max must have recognized Kyle's name, because he stood up from his spot on the ground, nudged his way between Carmen and Chuy, and positioned himself in front of Justin's legs. If Emilio made a move toward Justin, he'd have to go through Max first.

Justin knew better than to take Emilio's bait, and kept his mouth shut. "Semper fi, man," Emilio went on, tapping his fist into his chest. "Kyle was the only dude on the wrestling squad who could take me down. I tried to get him to do business with me, too, but he turned me down. I've got a feeling maybe we would've had trouble when he came back, so maybe it's for the best, no?"

Justin's hands curled into fists, and he took a step forward. He felt Max leaning against his legs, stopping him from going any farther, and a firm hand was placed on his shoulder. "Justin," Carmen whispered from behind him, "No. He's not worth it."

Justin exhaled. He knew he should listen to Carmen, but it was hard for him to let anyone—especially this guy—talk about Kyle that way.

"Am I right?" Emilio asked, his fake smile suddenly turned menacing.

"If you say so," Justin said through gritted teeth.

"I *do* say so. I also say that you've got some nerve asking me for an extra two hundred for that last game you ripped."

"If it's not worth it, don't buy it," Justin replied, his voice heavy with sarcasm.

Emilio looked at Chuy. "You hear that, Chuy? You could pick up some attitude tips from this kid." Emilio turned his gaze on Carmen as if he were just noticing her for the first time. "Who's this?"

"My cousin," Chuy said anxiously.

"Your cousin? *I'm* your cousin. I don't know her," Emilio said, glaring at Carmen. Carmen put her hands on her hips and stared Emilio down. It was clear she didn't like this guy one bit.

"On my mother's side," Chuy replied, starting to sound truly unhappy. But Justin wasn't sorry to see Chuy squirm. His friend deserved it for setting this up with Emilio.

"Guess all the looks are on my side of the family," Emilio said, a nasty smile crossing his face.

Justin wanted to go for him again, but Carmen kept a grip on his shoulder. She didn't flinch. She scowled at Emilio until he looked away with a careless laugh.

Emilio's phone buzzed in his pocket. "Yo, Tyler, what's up?" he said as he answered it.

Justin and Carmen exchanged a glance. *Tyler?* It could only be one person, and what did he have to do with this?

"No stress, man," Emilio said into his phone. "My people and I will be there. I'm on my way." Emilio slipped the phone back into his pocket, then took a couple of steps forward, stopping just a few inches from Justin. Emilio loomed over him and looked right down into his face. "*Total Combat 4* comes out next week, kid. You rip that for me—at the regular rate—and we're good." Emilio's tone turned dark on the last words.

Max jumped up and nosed between Justin and Emilio. A low, deep growling sound came from his throat. Justin felt Max's furry head rubbing against his hand. Emilio looked down at Max.

"Oh yeah, I heard about you, dog. You tore up a bunch of Navy Seals at the church. Tough guy, huh?" Emilio raised his hands in a fake surrender gesture, turned away, and started to climb into his truck.

Justin's blood was boiling, and his heart pounded like a hammer. He was starting to put two and two together. Based on the conversation he'd just overheard, it sounded as if Tyler and Emilio were doing *something* together. He still hadn't figured out what Tyler was up to, but whatever it was, it definitely wasn't good if it involved Emilio. Justin shook his head. How had his brother ever been best friends with a guy like Tyler?

Justin suddenly had a crazy idea and didn't want to miss his chance.

"Pay me up front," he called after Emilio, sounding more confident than he felt.

Emilio turned back and glared at Justin. "What did you say?"

"I said pay me up front for the game."

Emilio cracked a huge, sinister smile. He pulled a roll of cash from his pocket and counted off a handful of bills. He dangled them in front of Justin's face. "I want the disc in my hand on Friday. You got it?"

Justin nodded. Emilio slapped the cash into his outstretched palm, hopped in his truck, and tore out of the driveway at top speed.

Justin turned on Chuy, furious about getting ambushed. "He just *happened* to be making the rounds?" Justin yelled. "What's your problem, man? You *told* him I was here."

Chuy looked miserable. "I'm sorry, J. He's just—he's been on me about that game, and I didn't know what to tell him."

Justin shook his head and started to walk away. He knew Chuy hadn't wanted to get him in trouble with Emilio, and he also knew how threatening Emilio could be. Justin had to admit that it was a tough spot to be in. He felt bad for Chuy, but he needed some time to cool down. He stopped and turned to Carmen. "Thanks for . . . for everything. I'll call you later, okay?"

She nodded.

"You mean, you would if you had a phone," Chuy said under his breath. Carmen punched him hard in the arm. Max let out a small *woof.*

"Ow," Chuy said, rubbing at the bruise.

Justin's brain was running on overdrive. Something hadn't felt right about Tyler from the moment he walked into their house the other night, and he was determined to figure out what it was. If that meant bringing Emilio down, too, then all the better.

But no matter how he figured it out, Justin couldn't get around the fact that Tyler was an ex-Marine, and bigger and stronger than he was. Plus he was pretty sure Emilio was packing a gun.

Justin needed to be careful. But most of all, for any of this to work, he needed to find the two men as quickly as possible. Fortunately, Justin had a secret weapon to help him—he had just watched a video of that very weapon in action, doing what he was trained to do.

After he'd left Chuy and Carmen behind at the house, Justin leaned down to Max and held out the stack of cash under his nose. "Okay, Max, buddy, let's see what you've got."

Max made a snuffling noise as he ran his nose over the money a few times. He looked up at Justin expectantly, his whole body tensed and ready for action. Justin stuffed the bills in his pocket, grabbed his bike, and hopped on.

"Okay, Max. *Go search!*"

Max took off like a shot, bolting down the street in the direction Emilio had gone. Justin rode hard, trying to keep up.

Whatever Emilio and Tyler were up to, he was going to get to the bottom of it.

SIXTEEN

JUSTIN BREATHED IN RHYTHM WITH HIS PEDALING. MAX ran at full speed about a hundred yards ahead. Justin couldn't believe the pace Max could keep up for so long. He moved so fast and so effortlessly—it was like he was barely even exerting himself. Justin, on the other hand, was getting a good workout. His side was cramping up, but he couldn't slow down now. He had to keep up with Emilio's truck.

Every once in a while, Max got too far ahead of Justin. Max would stop and wait for him to catch up, his tongue hanging out of his mouth. Justin was pretty sure that if Max could talk, he'd be telling him to hurry up.

Max led Justin through a part of town he'd never been in before. For a minute, Justin thought Max was going to stop in front of one of the dilapidated houses or empty storefronts, but he didn't. He just barreled forward, down one street and then another, until finally he stopped at the end of a block, where the asphalt gave way to a dirt path. He sniffed excitedly at the ground.

Justin pulled up to a stop.

"What's the matter, boy?" he asked as he caught his breath. "Did you lose him?"

Max raised his head and sniffed at the air for a second. Justin could tell from the twitch of his nose and the way his head tilted a little this way, then a little that way, that he was sorting through the hundreds of things he could smell all at once.

Suddenly, Max locked onto a scent. He hopped up and took off again, forging into the woods. Justin raced after him.

They barreled through dense foliage and over a rutted, narrow dirt road that Justin had never been on before. The trees were so thick overhead that very little sunlight came through. The path was shaded and treacherous. There were rocks and roots everywhere, and Justin had to focus to keep from getting thrown from his bike. Max moved almost silently over the undergrowth and dirt—it was like he floated when he ran.

After what seemed like forever, Max finally stopped. He crouched down and raised his snout in the air. His ears stood at attention, pointing right for the sky. Every inch of his body was alert and ready. He stayed like that until Justin pulled up next to him and stopped. Max was scanning the trees, his ears and nose tuning in to frequencies of sound and scents Justin would never know. Justin couldn't believe how cool it was to see Max's training at work.

Justin heard voices through the trees. He couldn't see any faces, but at least one of the men sounded familiar—he could hear Emilio's voice drifting toward him.

"Should we do the smart thing and get out of here?" Justin whispered to Max. Max turned his big brown eyes to Justin and held his gaze for a moment. He panted, then snapped his mouth shut. Justin smiled. "Nah, I don't think so, either." He scratched the top of Max's head. "Good job, buddy."

Suddenly, Max's ears pricked forward, and his head whipped around to the direction they had come.

Before Justin could wonder what was happening, he felt a rumble in the ground and heard the sound of an engine approaching, fast. Someone was coming right for them, along the road they had just traveled.

Justin hopped off his bike and dragged it off to the side of the road. He grabbed Max by the collar and led him into the foliage. They crouched down, side by side, behind a fallen tree, just seconds before a 4x4 truck with massive off-road tires sped down the road and passed right by them. Justin got a quick glimpse through the side window: Tyler sat in the passenger seat, a serious look on his face. He couldn't tell who was driving.

Max tried to pull away, but Justin held him tightly by the collar. He put a finger on Max's nose.

"Shhhhh, Max," Justin whispered. "Stay."

The truck disappeared over a small slope. Justin heard it downshift, then come to a stop. Justin and Max crept slowly forward until they could see over the rise and down into a clearing below.

Emilio stood with a small group of extremely scary-looking dudes. They had huge biceps and wore matching leather jackets and tall, black leather boots. One of them—the smallest guy—seemed to be in charge. He was giving directions in Spanish.

Tyler hopped out of the truck, while the largest man Justin had ever seen emerged out of the driver's side. He was well over six feet tall, and he was as wide as three other men put together. He loomed over Tyler. Justin could see why he'd brought him along. He wore jeans, a leather vest, and had a very obvious holster on his belt.

The giant man whistled sharply, and two sturdy Rottweilers sailed out of the back of the truck, their muscles rippling in the sunlight. They landed on the ground with a *thud*, and sat down, one on either side of Tyler and the man. Max shifted his weight and whimpered softly. Justin instinctively put an arm around Max's neck, hoping it would settle him.

"Stack, show them," Tyler snapped. The humongous man, Stack, lumbered around to the back of the truck, the dogs trailing closely behind him, and opened the doors. He lifted out a long metal object.

It took a second for Justin to realize what he was seeing—it was a military rifle. Kyle had once shown him something like it on a video call. Stack handed it over to Emilio's buddy. The man inspected it carefully. He raised it to his shoulder and pointed it into the woods near Justin and Max.

Justin's heart was pounding so hard, he was sure the

men would be able to hear it. Max licked his lips and tried to pull away. His instincts were kicking in—after all, he was trained to find weapons just like that one. Justin held him tightly.

The man holding the rifle spoke in Spanish to Emilio. Justin couldn't understand the words, but he knew the tone wasn't exactly friendly.

"He likes it," Emilio said to Tyler, "but he wants to know for sure you've got more where this came from."

"I understood what he said," Tyler said sharply. "Tell him this is strictly show-and-tell. There's plenty more."

The man spoke to Emilio in Spanish again.

"He wants to know where the rest is," Emilio translated.

Tyler smirked. "It's stored in a nice, safe place. We'll deliver it as soon as the second half of the money is deposited into my account. *Like we agreed upon.*" Tyler's voice was laden with menace. He stepped forward and snatched the weapon back from the man's hand. "That'll take down a chopper," he said with a grin. "But if you *really* want to do some damage, check this one out." Tyler snapped his fingers at Stack, who stomped over to the back of the truck and pulled out a bigger, heavier, and altogether scarier-looking weapon.

Justin recognized it immediately as a rocket launcher—something else Kyle had taught him about.

Justin swallowed hard. This was serious business. He and Max needed to get out of here, fast. He was getting in way over his head, and it seemed like the best idea was to alert the authorities that something super illegal was about to go down.

Just as Justin was about to pull Max back toward the road, Max caught the scent of the rocket launcher. Justin recalled that the last big haul Max and Kyle had found before Kyle was killed was a huge cache of weapons—just like this one. Before Justin could stop him, Max's entire demeanor changed. He stood up on all fours. His eyes lit up, his ears pointed forward, his mouth snapped shut, and he whimpered loudly. Justin's stomach flipped, and adrenaline shot through his body. *This wasn't good.*

Sure enough, one of the Rottweilers—the bigger, meaner-looking one—heard Max and snapped to attention. Both of Stack's dogs now skittered excitedly around the clearing, sniffing at the air, their muscular bodies poised for action. They both started to growl as they nosed at the underbrush.

This was bad, Justin thought. Very, very bad.

Tyler whispered something to Stack, who tried to get his dogs in line with a few commands. The man with Emilio had taken note of the dogs' behavior, too, and started to speak nervously in Spanish. Emilio gave a concerned nod as he listened.

"He wants to know what's bothering the dogs," Emilio said.

"Probably just some critter," Stack said. "A coyote, maybe."

"Still," Tyler said smoothly, "no reason to hang around here any longer than we need to, right? Your boy good, Emilio?"

Emilio and the man exchanged a few words in Spanish.

"The money will be wired into your account in the morning." Emilio took one step forward and got in Tyler's face. He pointed a finger at Tyler. "But if you're setting him up—"

Tyler swatted Emilio's hand away. "No one's setting anyone up. You tell him that." Tyler stared down Emilio until Emilio turned away and hopped in a huge black SUV with the three other men. They sped out of the clearing, leaving a trail of dust.

Tyler turned to Stack, a look of fury on his face. "Send those dogs out, *now*!"

Stack whistled, and with a great flurry of barking and growling, the Rottweilers bounded toward the trees.

They were coming for Justin and Max.

SEVENTEEN

JUSTIN RAN FASTER THAN HE HAD EVER RUN IN HIS LIFE. He had never had a reason to move that quickly before, because he'd never been chased by two rabid beasts and two men with guns.

He could hear the burly Rottweilers tromping through the underbrush and panting heavily as they came after him and Max. Justin reached his bike and grabbed the handlebars. He hopped on and was just about to take off when the smaller of the two dogs came bursting through the trees.

The Rottweiler blocked their path and growled at Justin. Before the huge dog could make a move, Max lunged at him, guarding Justin. The two dogs snarled at each other, their upper lips curling up to reveal their fangs. The Rottweiler seemed to hesitate, and for a second Justin thought maybe they could get around him and get out of there.

Suddenly, the second Rottweiler came charging out of the woods. He leaped into the air, heading right for Justin. Justin raised his arm to protect himself, but Max hurtled himself at the dog, slamming into the Rottweiler in midair and knocking him to the ground. Max landed on top of him. The two dogs rolled around in the dirt, a frenzy of growls and bites and scratches, battling each other fiercely. Justin watched helplessly, unable to tell if Max was getting hurt.

Max pulled back from the Rottweiler, his sides heaving as he panted, and the dogs circled each other for a long moment. Justin held his breath, trying desperately to think of some way to help Max. He looked around for a large rock, but couldn't find anything. Max looked up at him, as if he was trying to tell Justin something. Before Justin had a chance to figure out what, Max suddenly zipped past him, running farther into the woods. The Rottweilers followed, nipping at his heels.

Max was leading the dogs away from Justin. *So Justin could escape.*

Justin was too worried about Max to move at first. He stood, frozen, watching the trees where Max had disappeared. Would Max be able to defend himself against two dogs? Would he know how to get home? Justin hated the thought of leaving Max behind in the woods. But Max had clearly wanted to give Justin a chance to get away.

Justin heard heavy footsteps moving through the trees. Then Tyler's voice drifted toward his hiding spot. He was yelling at Stack. "That was no coyote. How could you let this happen?"

Justin didn't wait around for Stack's response. He hopped on his bike and spun off down the road that led out of the woods. He pedaled furiously over the bumps and dips, barely steering around knotty patches of vines and roots.

He took a chance and turned to look behind him for a second, to see if anyone was catching up. Just as he did, Justin hit something with his front tire, and flew up and over his handlebars, landing flat on his back. The wind was knocked out of him, and he lay there for a split second, trying to breathe again. His entire body was in shock from the sudden pain. Justin stood up carefully and gingerly decided he wasn't seriously hurt, maybe just a few scrapes and bruises.

His bike, on the other hand, was completely destroyed. The front rim was totally mangled, and the tire was flat as a pancake. But there was no time to feel sorry for himself or be sad about the bike that he and Kyle used to work on together. The bike they had tuned up while Tyler watched—Tyler, the same man who was chasing Justin that very second.

Justin picked up his bike and tossed it off to the side of the road, into a thick patch of leaves. He'd have to come back for it later. Then he took off on foot.

Justin didn't know what was worse: Hearing Tyler and Stack chasing after him, or hearing nothing at all. The woods were still as he ran along. He couldn't even hear Max's barking anymore, and he hoped that his dog was safe. After a few minutes, Justin realized he had somehow gotten off the dirt road and onto a smaller path. He must have taken a wrong turn somewhere. Now he had even less of a clue where he was—or how to get out of here.

A whooshing sound suddenly broke through the quiet. It was silent again for a moment, then *whoosh*—he heard it again. Cars. He was hearing cars driving by. Justin hurried in the direction of the noise, and let out a whoop when he stumbled out of the trees and onto the side of a paved two-lane road. It was empty of cars. As he waited for someone to drive by, he heard a rustling sound behind him. He spun around, ready to fight, but instead dropped to his knees.

Max!

He was alive. Injured and limping, with blood on his side, but very much alive.

A car appeared in the distance.

"Lie down, Max," Justin said. Max lay down.

The sedan cruised along toward them, and Justin stepped into the middle of the road, waving his arms frantically over his head. The car came to a stop, and an old lady rolled down the passenger-side window. She looked like she could be someone's grandma.

"Are you okay, son?" she asked worriedly.

"I'm fine, ma'am, but my dog is hurt. We need a ride," Justin begged.

"Well, hop in," she said, motioning for him to get inside.

Justin opened the back door for Max. They were both surprised to hear a burst of high-pitched barks and yips. Justin leaned in to see a small, fluffy white dog, bouncing around frantically on the backseat. The dog glared at Max. Max hesitated for a second, taking in the tiny terror. Justin looked over his shoulder to see if Stack or Tyler were coming. They weren't. Yet. But they would pick up Justin's trail soon enough.

"Let's go, Max," Justin urged. "Up."

Max clambered into the backseat, and Justin sat in the front. The little dog continued its frenzied yapping. Max ignored it and stared out the window.

"Ma'am, may I borrow your phone?" Justin asked. It was the millionth time in his life that he wished he had a cell phone.

"Sure, honey." She dug around for it in her purse.

Justin smiled at her and off they drove—away from the Rottweilers, away from Stack, and, most important, away from Tyler.

EIGHTEEN

CHUY'S EYES LOOKED AS IF THEY WERE GOING TO POP out of his head.

"Four hundred and fifty dollars?" he repeated, astonished.

"And forty-seven cents," said the woman behind the counter at the emergency veterinarian's office.

"For dog stitches?" Chuy asked. "I'd hate to hear what you charge for a human."

"Chuy," Carmen said from where she was kneeling next to Max, "the important thing is that Max is okay."

Max's head was framed by a wide plastic cone that had been attached to his neck. It was to keep him from licking at his wounds while they healed, but it made him look like an alien. Carmen ran her hand over Max's head and gave him a gentle scratch behind the ears. "Right, Max?"

Justin nudged Chuy aside and arranged his facial features into what he hoped were a pathetic, helpless expression.

"Ma'am, I'm sorry. Can you give us a second?" he said to the receptionist.

The woman nodded.

Justin turned to Chuy. "How much did your mom give you?" he asked.

"'Give me'?" Chuy said. "She didn't *give* me jack. This is my life savings."

"Your life savings is a hundred dollars?" Justin said before he could stop himself.

Chuy looked insulted. "You don't want it, man, that's cool with me."

"No—no, that's not what I meant," Justin backpedaled. "Sorry. Yes, thank you, I'll take it."

Justin took the cash Chuy reluctantly handed over. He added it to the two hundred he had in his pocket from Emilio. He handed it to the woman, who just shook her head.

"I'm sorry. We can't release Max without full payment. I'm going to have to call your parents."

"Please, ma'am—don't do that," Justin pleaded. "I'm good for the rest, I promise. I'll give you my phone number and home address so you can find me. I just need time to figure out what to tell my dad, that's all." He paused for effect and tried the sad face again. "Please?"

She pursed her lips and studied him for a moment. Finally, she nodded and took the money from his hand. "Okay."

Justin exhaled a sigh of relief. "Thank you so much," he said. Then, turning to Chuy and Carmen, he said under his breath, "What *am* I going to tell my dad?"

"If this has anything to do with Emilio," Chuy cautioned as they headed for the parking lot, Max walking gingerly between them, "then nothing."

"I can't do that," Justin replied.

Chuy stepped in front of him and stopped him in his tracks. "J., listen to me. That dude is crazy. Family doesn't mean anything to him—and you're not even family. Trust me."

Justin didn't say anything.

"Fine," Chuy added. "But if you care about me and Carmen at all, leave us out of it."

★ ★ ★

EXHAUSTED, JUSTIN AND MAX HEADED UP THE DRIVEway toward the backyard. Justin had never been so happy to be home. From the looks of it, Max felt the same way. The moment they stepped into the yard, though, Max started barking like crazy. Justin led him to his cage and nudged him inside.

"What's up, pal?" Justin asked in surprise.

Max growled and yelped some more. Justin didn't have any choice but to shut the cage door and lock it. "You just need some rest, Max. We both do," he said.

Justin headed inside as Max continued making lots of noise. The barking was setting Justin on edge—although he was already pretty tense. Justin knew that he couldn't let Tyler and Emilio go through with the sale of those guns without trying to stop it. But there was no doubt in his mind that Tyler and Stack—not to mention Emilio and those scary Spanish-speaking dudes—would hurt whoever tried to get in their way. As far as Justin could tell, he only had one thing going for him, at least for the moment: They didn't know it had been him and Max in the woods.

It was a dangerous situation, and Justin wasn't sure what to do. He should probably call the sheriff or something.

He stepped inside his house through the sliding back door. It was weirdly quiet. Normally his mom was home by now, cooking dinner, but she wasn't in the kitchen. Nothing was on the stove.

"Mom?" he called out.

"In here, Justin," his mom responded. Her voice sounded funny.

Justin stepped into the living room and found his mom perched on the couch, looking upset. Next to her, with a smug look on his face, sat Tyler. Fear shot through Justin's body, and he looked away from Tyler. He wanted to turn around, grab Max, and bolt, but he couldn't.

"What have you done, Justin?" Justin's mom asked in a stern voice. He could tell she was torn between disappointment and worry.

"What have I done?" he asked, genuinely confused.

"Tyler told me what Max did to the deputy sheriff's dog," she replied.

Tyler tilted his head ever so slightly, his eyes locking on Justin, as he waited for him to reply. Justin could still hear Max barking in the yard—this was what his dog had been trying to warn him about.

"I don't know what he's talking about," Justin said.

It was the truth. His mind raced, trying to catch up with this information. He knew Tyler was trying to pull something, but he couldn't figure out what any deputy sheriff had to do with it. Then Justin had the odd sensation that someone was watching him from behind. He turned slowly to see Stack—dressed in a tan sheriff's uniform, a shiny metal badge pinned to his barrel chest, a service revolver hanging from a leather belt slung around his hips—lurking in the corner of his living room. The man's head practically touched the ceiling, he was so tall and wide. Justin's blood went cold, and his palms got clammy. Max was still yowling away outside.

Stack nodded at him. Justin noticed that one of his giant, meaty hands was wrapped in a bloody bandage. Justin couldn't help but hope that Max had inflicted that wound, and that it was a particularly nasty one.

"Don't lie to me, Justin." His mom's voice was quiet but steady. It was the way she sounded when she was really, really angry. "Don't you dare lie."

Stack stepped forward, his eyes fixed on Justin. His whole demeanor had changed from just a few hours earlier—he was in full sheriff mode now. So much for calling the authorities, Justin thought. *Stack was the authorities.*

"There I was, just having a few off-duty beers with my buddy Tyler," Stack said, "when *wham!* one of my dogs gets pounced on by *your* dog." He tipped his head menacingly toward Justin. "My poor Rottweiler didn't know what hit him." He held up his bandaged hand. "Your dog got me pretty good, too, when I tried to break it up." Stack took another step toward Justin. Justin forced himself to stay put. "I had to put him down. My *own* dog." Stack paused—he looked upset. Was it possible the monster actually had feelings? "What your animal did—that's assault, son. The law says that your family is liable for whatever he does, but I'll drop any charges if you just put him down now."

Justin struggled to keep his expression neutral. Stack and Tyler were both lying, and worse, his mom believed them. His nostrils flared as he tried to steady his breathing and get his emotions under control. He wasn't going to let anything happen to Max, no matter what Stack and Tyler had to say about it.

"The truth is," Stack said, lowering his voice, "he's going to be put down either way."

Justin swallowed hard. Max moved on from barking to howling.

"Max wasn't near you or your dogs," Justin said, hoping he sounded more certain than he felt.

Neither Stack nor Tyler responded. Instead, Stack stepped into the foyer and returned, clutching Justin's mangled bike in one hand. It looked like a toy in his massive grip.

"Found this bike near my place," Stack said. "It's yours, isn't it?"

Justin cursed silently.

"Well, Justin—is it?" Justin's mom demanded.

What could Justin say that would make all this go away? His mind leaped from one option to the next, but for once, he couldn't think of anything that would make this better. Anything he said could only make it worse.

Tyler stood up from the couch. "Justin," Tyler said in the fake friendly voice he always used whenever Kyle and Justin's parents were around, "why don't you and I go have a little talk in the other room, man to man?"

Tyler turned and gave Justin's mom a smile and nod, as if to reassure her that he could be Justin's big brother in Kyle's absence. Her eyes filled with tears, and she smiled gratefully at Tyler. Justin wanted to kick the man in the shins, but he followed him upstairs to his bedroom instead. Max was still barking and yelping like a maniac outside.

Tyler shut Justin's bedroom door firmly behind him. He pulled a massive gun from his waistband and held it up, waving it in front of Justin.

"Know what this is, kid?"

Justin didn't answer.

"This is a really, really nice gun. Know how much it's worth?"

Again, Justin said nothing.

"Around here, six hundred bucks at the mall. Know what it's worth over the border, in Mexico?"

Justin waited. He stared at the wall over Tyler's shoulder. He wasn't going to let Tyler intimidate him, even if that gun made him pretty nervous.

"Just a shade over three *thousand* dollars." Tyler stashed the gun in the back waistband of his jeans again, under his jacket. "Kyle wouldn't give Emilio the time of day, you know. But I do business with him." Tyler stepped forward until he was just inches from Justin, looming over him. "And so do you."

Justin cringed. He shouldn't have been surprised that Tyler knew he sold bootlegged video games to Emilio, but he was.

"That's right," Tyler said, clearly enjoying Justin's reaction. "Kyle and I found out about your little side business on our last leave. Kyle was going to tell your dad, but I talked him out of it. Word of honor. See, kid, you and I are more alike than you and Kyle ever were."

The suggestion that he and Tyler had anything in common filled Justin with disgust and rage. It took every ounce of self-control he had to keep from punching Tyler in the face. But Justin knew that, as good as it would feel for a split second, it would only cause more trouble in the end.

"Why don't you leave Max out of it?" Justin finally said.

"If it was up to me," Tyler said, his voice oozing with insincerity, "believe me I would. But Stack is steaming mad at your dog, and you don't want to mess with him when he's mad. That is one bad man down there. And the guys we're in business with? They're even badder." Tyler grinned, like the danger was part of the fun. Then his voice took on an ominous tone. "You want front-row seats at a couple more family funerals?"

Tyler's words sank into Justin's brain. *He was threatening Justin's parents.* Justin locked eyes with Tyler.

"That's right, kid," Tyler went on. "Stack knows where you live now. He knows who your parents are. Things go bad on this deal, and I'm sure he won't be shy about telling our business partners who's responsible for that." He poked Justin hard in the chest with one finger, but Justin didn't budge. "I might not like it, but I can't say that I'd blame him. Business is business, right?" Tyler leaned down until he and Justin were nose to nose. "Your mom and dad are like family to me, kid. So do us all a favor, and keep your mouth shut."

Justin kept his gaze zeroed in on Tyler. After a moment, he mustered up the ability to speak. "Did Kyle know about your 'business'?"

"*My* business? I'm just a little fish in a big pond." Tyler's tone had taken on a hint of disdain, like he was being forced to explain something obvious to a child. "The big fish sell weapons all over the world and make a lot of money doing it. Then they send wide-eyed hicks like me and Kyle out there to get shot at with those very same weapons, so they can cry big crocodile tears, salute the flag, and sell some more."

Tyler paused, and Justin struggled to absorb what he'd heard. He couldn't bear the image of Kyle getting shot by weapons just like the ones Tyler was selling to Emilio's guys.

"Kyle wanted to be a hero," Tyler went on. "Look where that got him." From the expression on Tyler's face, he knew he had hit a nerve with Justin. "Me? I'm a realist. I know how the world *really* works." He steadied his gaze on Justin. "Which one are you gonna be?"

★ ★ ★

JUSTIN COULDN'T BELIEVE HOW QUICKLY THE ANIMAL control guys got to the house. He yanked on Max's leash, practically dragging the reluctant dog to the curb. A van idled at the bottom of the driveway, its back doors opened wide to reveal a large metal crate. Two handlers with long metal poles stood on either side of the van. At the end of each pole was a soft loop, for corralling a wild dog around the neck.

Max was *not* a wild dog. He whimpered at Justin's side, but reluctantly obeyed. He tried to dig his paws into the ground, but his claws just slipped along the concrete. It broke Justin's heart to watch him struggle.

He couldn't explain to Max what was happening—he just had to hope that in some small way, Max understood. Justin would never be able to forgive himself for sacrificing Kyle's dog—his dog—this way. But he would never be able to *live* if anything happened to his parents. He didn't have a choice.

Stack, Tyler, and Justin's mom stood by the front

door, watching from a distance. Justin and Max reached the van, and Max tried even harder to pull away.

"Come on, Max," Justin commanded. "Be a good boy. Up."

It was almost as if Max just gave up. At the sound of Justin's voice, his whole body went slack, and he stopped fighting. He hopped into the van and slinked into the crate, his head and tail hanging low. Justin felt as though his heart was cracking into two pieces, seeing the dog behind bars.

"I'm sorry, Max," he choked out, his voice breaking. Tears filled his eyes. "You deserve better than this. I just—I don't know what else to do. Please understand."

Justin stepped back, struggling to keep it together in front of all these people. He turned to one of the handlers.

"How long before—until you—" He couldn't finish the sentence.

The man gave him a sympathetic look. "Forty-eight hours," he said. Then he shut the van doors with a heavy thump.

He couldn't watch the van pull away—it was too much. Justin pushed past Tyler, Stack, and his mother and headed into the house. He slammed the front door behind him. He looked out the window and saw Tyler putting his arm around his mom's shoulders, comforting her. Tyler was a snake—a dangerous, scheming, lying snake—and there was nothing he could do about it. Justin felt as defeated as Max.

Justin's busted-up bike lay in the middle of the living room. He kicked at it in frustration, stomping on the spokes until they cracked, wishing desperately that he was kicking at Tyler's head. Suddenly, it became crystal clear to Justin what he needed to help him out of this situation: He needed Kyle. Kyle would know what to do. Kyle would know what to say. Kyle wouldn't be so scared that he'd back down and send Max off to die.

Justin let out an angry yell as he destroyed what was left of his tires.

He was interrupted by the ringing phone. He ignored it, until the answering machine picked up, and he heard a familiar voice on the line.

"Hello, Mr. and Mrs. Wincott, this is Sergeant Reyes, over at Maitland. I—"

Justin stormed into the kitchen and snatched the phone from the cradle. "Hello?" he said.

"Hi, Justin? Is that you? It's Sergeant Reyes. I have

some information for you—I followed up on what we talked about when you were here, and—"

Justin had nearly forgotten about their last conversation. Now it was too late, and too dangerous, to do anything about it. "Sergeant, I don't think—" he started to say before Reyes cut him off.

"Justin, this is important," Reyes said. "Tyler Harne's service record is officially protected by privacy laws. But I talked to some people, and I want to tell your parents—"

"No!" Justin interrupted him. "No way."

"Son, this is serious business I'm talking about here. No one could prove anything, but Harne was busted for falsifying field reports. You told me he's been lying to your father. I just want to tell your parents. They deserve to know, Justin."

Justin started to panic. If Reyes told his parents about Tyler's lies, then his dad would confront Tyler, for sure. And nothing good would come of that—his mom and dad would be in real danger. He had to stop Reyes from telling them anything.

"If you tell my parents," Justin said, trying to sound as forceful as he could, "I'll tell your bosses you gave me a confidential training video."

Reyes was silent on the other end of the line.

"Justin," he finally said, his voice laced with concern. "Are you all right?"

"I'll tell them you gave me even more classified stuff, but I threw it away because I was scared of getting in trouble. I mean it. I'll swear to it."

"Justin—" Reyes pleaded.

"Don't call here again," Justin snapped before hanging up the phone.

NINETEEN

HOURS LATER, JUSTIN SAT IN HIS ROOM, HIS STOMACH growling with hunger. He had skipped dinner that night, and his parents had left him alone. There was no way he would have been able to eat after watching Max be driven away to meet his fate. He also didn't want to face his mom and dad. So he'd holed up in his room, trying desperately to think of a way to save Max without putting his family in danger. Time after time, he had come up empty-handed.

Now it was late, and Justin was starving. He stepped out into the quiet of the hall, preparing to sneak down to the kitchen—only his parents were still awake. He heard them talking in soft voices downstairs, so he stopped at the top of the stairs to listen.

"This isn't sitting right," his dad said. "That deputy's place is a long way off. What was Justin doing out there with Max anyway?"

"I don't know," his mom replied. "He won't tell me. You want to know what's happening with Justin, you'll need to ask him yourself. It's about time you did."

"I could talk to Kyle." His dad sounded sad. "But Justin, I don't know. It's like I don't even know my own son."

His words were like a punch to Justin's gut. He had never heard his dad sound so . . . regretful before. Justin had always thought his dad didn't *want* to know him, but maybe that wasn't true.

"You want to know your own son?" his mom asked, her voice firm. "Then turn around and look in the mirror. You two are more alike than either one of you will ever care to admit. I've been keeping the peace in this house since the day Kyle shipped out." She was silent for a moment, as if letting her words sink in. "I've already lost one son, Ray. If it's all right with you, I'd very much like to hold on to the other."

Justin heard his dad sigh, then push back his chair

and walk heavily across the living room. He was coming upstairs to talk to Justin.

Justin scrambled back to his room and shut the door just before his dad reached the top of the stairs. He threw himself onto his bed and picked up a comic book. A moment later, there was a soft knock on his door. His dad entered without waiting for an invitation. Justin looked up at him. His dad stood in the doorway looking awkward, like he often did when he was trying to talk about anything that might involve feelings. Justin almost felt bad for him.

"Justin, I—" His dad stopped, collected himself, then started again. "Is there anything else you want to tell me about what happened with Max today?"

Justin swallowed hard. *Everything*. That's what he wanted to tell his dad—everything, from start to finish. He didn't even care how much trouble he got in. But there was no way he could tell his dad even one word about Tyler. Because if he did, he'd get them all killed.

"I'm sorry," Justin managed to choke out.

His dad looked surprised to hear Justin apologize.

"That's not what I meant," his dad said.

It was Justin's turn to be surprised. If his dad wasn't

here to get him in trouble, then what did he want to talk about?

His dad furrowed up his brow and studied Justin for a long moment.

"Son, I've seen you make a lot of trouble. I've also always seen you own up to it. Until now."

Even though Justin and his father had never gotten along, there was no denying that his dad was always able to tell when something serious was up. It was uncanny, really. And for once in his life, Justin actually wanted his dad to figure it out, to tell him what to do, but he couldn't risk it. He had to throw him off course.

"Guess I'm not a hero, like you and Kyle." Justin lowered his eyes back to his reading. "That's the way it goes, I guess."

He expected his dad to get angry, like usual, but he didn't. Instead he took one limping step closer to his bed. Justin looked up at him again. There was an unfamiliar look in his dad's eye—it was nice, friendly. Almost like he wanted to connect with Justin, rather than punish him.

"No one in this family has ever been drafted, son," his dad began. "Not my dad, not his. They enlisted. We all enlisted. WWII, Korea. Both of them were decorated soldiers. I signed up the day I turned eighteen." He paused, as if he was about to say something difficult. "In '91, I was deployed with my unit to Saudi Arabia. Desert Storm—the first Gulf War." His dad shook his head a little, almost sheepishly. "You know all that already." He paused, then continued.

"It was my first command. Day one, we're sent over the berm. An hour into Kuwait, we came up on the Al-Burqan oil field. The Iraqis had set it on fire, and there was smoke everywhere. Our eyes were burning—you couldn't even see your hand in front of your face. Then shots went off." He stopped again, looking like he was replaying the scene in his mind. "So we returned fire. Only, it turns out, we were firing on nobody. Because the shots were coming from *behind* us."

Justin's head shot up, and he stared at his dad with wide eyes. Was he saying what he thought he was saying?

"Friendly fire," his dad confirmed. "The enemy was long gone, but no one could see a thing, so our own guys were shooting at us. Accidentally. The guy next to me went down. I moved toward him, to help him. Then I got hit. I took two bullets in my leg. One passed through the muscle, but the other"—he tapped at his calf—"cracked right into my shinbone and shattered it like glass. I was helicoptered to Germany the next day. The war was over so fast, most of my guys got home before I did."

Justin was speechless. He'd always thought that his dad had seen serious action and been hurt in battle. Real battle, against the real enemy. But now that he thought about it, he'd never actually heard his dad say that. He'd only heard *other* people say it about his dad.

"By the time I got back," his dad went on, his gaze cast down at the rug, "people were telling all kinds of crazy stories. I tried to straighten them out, to tell the real story." He shook his head, ashamed. "But I could see how much it disappointed them." He looked back up at Justin. "How much they wanted to believe I was . . ." He trailed off. "Well, anyway, I stopped correcting them, sooner than I care to admit."

Justin and his dad sat in strained silence for a moment.

"I always wanted to tell Kyle. But when I saw the way he looked up to me—the way he looked at me . . . I just couldn't." His dad took a deep breath and exhaled slowly. He looked almost relieved, like he'd been wanting to get these words off his chest for a long time. "My point is, Justin, a hero tells the truth, no matter what people might think about him. And you've always done that. From day one."

Justin's eyes filled with hot tears at his father's words, but he willed them not to spill over onto his cheeks. He'd never heard praise from him before. He wanted nothing more than to tell his dad that he didn't care what had happened in Saudi Arabia—that he still looked up to him. That he still loved him. But Justin couldn't allow himself to speak. The stakes were too high. He couldn't afford to utter even one bad word about Tyler.

"If what happened to you and Max today is different from what Tyler and that deputy are saying, Justin, then I need to know about it." His dad was practically pleading.

Justin looked down at his comic book. "Dad, I'm gonna go to sleep now, okay?"

His dad looked as if he'd been slapped. He blinked a couple of times and took one step backward, as if he were catching his balance. Justin felt a sharp twinge in his chest, but steeled himself. He was keeping his mouth shut for everyone's good.

Without a word, his dad turned and left the room, closing the door behind him. From his bed, Justin heard the front door open, then slam shut.

★ ★ ★

A COUPLE OF HOURS LATER, JUSTIN WOKE WITH A START to the sound of the house phone ringing. The lights were still on in his bedroom. His comic book lay facedown on his chest. His neck ached from sleeping sitting up. He had fallen asleep while he was reading. He checked the clock—it was midnight.

He heard his mom's muffled voice downstairs, talking to someone on the phone. The conversation was short.

"Justin!" she called up.

Justin sat up and rubbed his eyes, trying to clear his groggy head.

"*Justin!*" she yelled again.

"I heard you, Mom," he said impatiently. "I'm coming." He hopped up and headed downstairs.

She stood in the kitchen, clutching the cordless phone and waving it in his direction. "What did you and your dad talk about earlier?"

"Nothing." He shrugged, still standing on the stairs.

"Well," she said, eyeing him suspiciously, "after you

talked about *nothing*, he stormed out of here without a word. I assumed he went to the office for something, but he's been gone for hours. And he just called to tell me not to worry, that everything's fine, but he's going to spend the night at our hunting cabin, and he's not sure when he'll be back."

A horrible thought dawned on Justin, but he told himself to remain calm.

"Do we have a hunting cabin?" he asked nervously.

"Not that I ever heard of," his mom said, her voice full of concern. "That's my point."

The knot of dread tightened in Justin's gut. A snippet of conversation—something Tyler had said to Emilio's guys in the clearing—nagged at him. He'd thought it was weird at the time, but after things went crazy, he'd forgotten about it. "*It's stored in a nice, safe place,*" Tyler had said about the weapons he was going to sell. He had to stash them somewhere safe, where no one would think to look. Like a storage space. *Like his dad's business.*

Justin and his mom locked eyes. There was so much he wished he could tell her.

His mom was worried enough without knowing about Tyler and the weapons. She turned from him and dialed 911. She spoke quickly and anxiously into the phone. Justin could tell from her side of the conversation that the police weren't going to do anything to help. His dad hadn't been missing long enough to warrant any kind of response, and he couldn't tell them what he knew. If the police tracked Tyler and his father down, sirens blaring, wouldn't Tyler know that Justin had ratted him out?

No, the only way to save his father was to find him by himself. But how?

His mom hung up the phone in tears. Justin wrapped her in a hug.

"He's fine, Mom," he said, though he didn't believe his own words. Justin had never felt more helpless—or hopeless—in his life. With no Kyle or Max to help him, how would he ever find his dad?

Just then, they were startled by a loud scratching noise at the back door. Before Justin had a chance to wonder what it was, he heard a familiar whimper, followed by a bark that made his heart soar. He had no idea how it could be possible, but there was no denying who was in their backyard.

It was Max.

TWENTY

JUSTIN BOUNCED HIS LEGS NERVOUSLY IN THE CAR. IT was hard to sit still, even for the short drive over to Chuy's house. His mom was an extremely cautious driver, which most of the time didn't bother him. But right now, he just wanted her to step on it.

They didn't speak. Justin was grateful that his mom was so distracted with worry about his dad that she didn't ask any questions. He'd simply explained that Chuy and Carmen might know something about where his dad had gone, and she had offered to drive him over. He just hoped they'd make it to Chuy's before she decided to be her usual curious self.

They pulled up out front. When Justin opened the car door the sound of a thousand yapping Chihuahuas floated over to them.

"I'll be right back," Justin said. "I just need to talk to them."

"Maybe I should come in with you," his mom said. "I still don't understand what Carmen and Chuy might know about your dad."

"Mom, please—I'll explain later. They're not going to talk to me with you there."

"Okay, but hurry back."

Justin hopped out, with Max following closely on his heels. Chuy answered the door, very surprised to see them. They stepped inside, and Max was instantly swarmed by tiny dogs.

Carmen hopped up from the couch with a worried look on her face. "Justin—is everything okay?"

"Can we talk outside?" Justin said to Chuy and Carmen in response. He didn't want to wake up the rest of Chuy's family. "Out back, I mean." Chuy gave a nod and led them through his living room. They stepped into the backyard.

"My dad's MIA," Justin said. There was no time to sugarcoat it. "He told my mom something weird about going to a hunting cabin, then just disappeared. The police don't care because he hasn't been missing for more than forty-eight hours yet."

"What's the big deal?" Chuy asked. "Maybe he's just working late or out with his friends or something."

Justin filled them in on Tyler and Stack's visit to his house, Tyler's threats, and Max's trip to Animal Control. Chuy's eyes grew wide, and Carmen chewed on her lip, deep in thought.

"What did you tell your mom you're doing here?" Carmen asked.

"I told her you guys knew something about what was going on," Justin replied apologetically.

"Uh, J., are you saying you lied to your mom about us?" Chuy slapped himself on the forehead. "Thanks a lot, man."

"I'm sorry, Chuy, but I needed to get here as fast as I could. And my bike is busted. Please—I need to find my dad. You don't have to do anything other than loan me a bike. And cover for me with my mom—I just need a five-minute head start. Okay?" Justin looked from Chuy to Carmen and back.

Without a word, Carmen stepped over to a bike leaning against the garage.

"Sure," she said with finality. "But I'm coming with you."

"No way." Justin shook his head. "This isn't your problem. It's mine." He couldn't bear the thought of dragging one more person into his mess. If anything happened to Carmen . . . He shook his head again.

"Are you going to waste time making an argument you're going to lose?" she asked him. "Or are you going to get on that bike?" She pointed at a second bike near hers.

"That's my bike," Chuy cut in. "And you can't have it."

Justin raised his hands in frustration. Hadn't Chuy just heard him explain that his father's life was in danger?

Chuy grinned. "You can't have it because I'll be riding it. Let's get a move on, people!"

"Chuy," Carmen interrupted, a skeptical look on her face, "I admire your enthusiasm, but are you expecting Justin to walk?"

The smirk fell from Chuy's face. He cast a nervous glance toward the house, then at a bike glistening in the moonlight a few feet away. It was a pristine Stumpjumper, with top-of-the-line rims and tires, a fancy cushioned seat, and a dozen of other custom extras. Justin knew it well.

"You can take my brother's bike," Chuy said, sounding like a man sealing his own doom. "But you know it's his prized possession. If you mess this thing up, you're going to have to save *my* life next."

"Deal." Justin nodded at his friends, grateful but nervous. He knew it was huge for Chuy to offer up his big brother's bike—*no one* touched that thing. If anything happened to it . . . if either of his friends got hurt . . . he wouldn't be able to live with himself.

Justin didn't want to put Carmen and Chuy in harm's way, but he was certainly happy to have their company.

"Let's go," Justin said. "We have to take the back way so my mom doesn't see us." He felt a twinge of guilt for abandoning her in Chuy's driveway with no explanation. Justin shuddered at the thought of the awkward conversation his mom was going to have with Chuy's parents in a few minutes—but by then he'd be long gone. She was going to be pretty angry when she realized that he'd taken off, but he was just trying to protect her. He wasn't going to take her anywhere near Tyler. He would just have to count on her understanding later, after his dad was back home, safe and sound.

Justin rode off into the darkness, with Carmen and Chuy right behind him. Max raced along beside them. They reached Open Range Storage in a few minutes, but Justin could tell right away the place was empty. The entire facility was dark and quiet. Still, he and Max rode between the rows of storage units, until they came to one with the door rolled up. The unit was bare. Max sniffed around it carefully, running his nose across the floor and along the perimeter. Justin spotted something in the far corner of the storage space. He leaned down to pick it up and recognized it immediately: It was his father's gun holster. And it was empty.

Adrenaline shot through Justin's body. They needed to move faster. He held the holster under Max's nose. Max's eyes lit up and his whole body started to vibrate with energy. This was what he was trained to do—this was what he was best at. He whimpered a little as he waited for Justin's orders.

"Max," Justin commanded. "*Go search!*"

★ ★ ★

JUSTIN SLOWED HIS BIKE TO A NEAR CRAWL AS HE approached the SUV in the parking lot at the edge of the woods. It was his father's truck. Max sniffed around its tires as Justin hopped off his bike and peered inside. The truck was abandoned, but when he felt the hood over the engine, it was still warm. His dad couldn't be that far ahead, unless they'd taken another car.

Chuy peered into the woods, a nervous look on his face. The forest was dark and pretty spooky at night.

"You having second thoughts?" Justin asked them.

Chuy shook his head. "My second thoughts are having second thoughts," he said. "But I'm good."

"Me too," Carmen said. "Let's go."

Max guided the way, following the scent to a dirt road that led into the woods. There were fresh tire tracks in the soft earth. Justin rode first, followed by his friends. The trees closed over their heads, and they could barely see the path in front of them. Moonlight occasionally peeked down through the branches, offering the only light on the dark road. The only sound Justin could hear was his own heavy breathing and the whirring of his bike tires.

They rode for what seemed like ages. The trees overhead began to thin out, and Justin could see dawn starting to lighten the sky. Finally, Max came to a halt at the edge of a rapidly moving river. Justin, Carmen, and Chuy came to a stop behind him. The river was at least a hundred yards across, and above them and to their left, the water dropped off over a steep waterfall, causing the current to churn and twist over rocks that jutted out at sharp angles.

"Oh, come *on*," Chuy said under his breath, looking up at the waterfall. Everything had just gone from bad to worse. It was going to be really tough to get across.

Max put his front paws into the water, then paused. He looked back at Justin.

"He's not going to do what I think he's going to do, is he?" Chuy groaned.

Max did. He hurtled his body forward into the water, paddling frantically against the rushing force of the water. Justin and Chuy exchanged a glance. Chuy shook his head but got off his bike and lifted it up over his head. Justin looked at Carmen, she nodded, and they did the same—hopping off their bikes and raising them over their heads. Chuy led the way, and the three of them resolutely waded right into the icy water.

Justin's skin felt like it was under attack. The water was so cold he actually felt paralyzed for a split second, and he had to stop moving until his body adjusted. His arms shook with the weight of the bike above him.

He looked at Carmen. She wore an expression of such fierce focus and determination; he almost had to smile at her.

They moved forward slowly, following Max's lead.

"I hope you guys know how to swim, by the way," Carmen half joked.

"I know how," Justin said, though it was pretty clear to him that swimming here would be a lot harder than doing it in the local pool.

"When did you ever swim?" Chuy asked, his face contorted with effort as he sloshed forward.

"It's just something you know how to do," Justin said, annoyed that Chuy would challenge him in front of Carmen.

"Whoa!" Chuy suddenly exclaimed. "It's getting deep right here. Watch out."

"If Max can do it, we ca—" Justin started to say, but his words were cut off as his feet slipped out from under him and he was sucked down into the water. The river closed over his head, flooding his nostrils and spinning him around in a circle.

He needed to use his arms to pull himself back up, or the current would carry him down the swift river. With no other choice, he dropped the Stumpjumper and swam wildly until he broke the surface. He gasped for air.

"Justin!" Carmen yelled. "Are you okay?"

"Justin, man, you scared me!" Chuy yelled.

"I dropped your brother's bike," Justin spluttered, coughing up water.

Chuy shook his head, as if to scold Justin. "I'd rather have you than that stupid bike. I got it. Just go ahead."

Chuy dropped his own bike and dove under the water. When he popped back up he was dragging his brother's bike behind him. Justin trudged forward, wading after Carmen. Max waited for them on the far bank, his ears perked up, looking anxious.

They pulled themselves onto the shore and collapsed with exhaustion and relief. They lay there panting and dripping for a moment, collecting themselves. Max licked Justin's face from left to right, top to bottom, and back again. Justin laughed and swatted him away.

"I'm okay, Max. I'm okay." He looked at Chuy. Justin never imagined his friend would do something like that for him. He held up his hand and Chuy high-fived him. "Thanks, man. I owe you one."

"No problem," Chuy said casually. "Just don't expect me to lick your face, and I think we're good."

"Ha." Suddenly Justin realized something. He sat up and looked into the water.

"Chuy—what about your bike?"

"We're not going back for it, if that's what you're thinking," Carmen said.

Chuy shrugged. "I needed a new one anyway."

Justin clapped his friend on the back in appreciation. "This was a terrible idea," Justin said. He buried his face in his hands.

"You think?" Chuy shot back. The three of them broke down into exhausted laughs.

Max's sharp bark brought them back to the business at hand. He was a few yards away, at the bottom of a steep hill. He spun in circles and wagged his tail, letting them know he was waiting for them to get up and follow him.

Justin sighed. He wasn't looking forward to pushing his bike up that huge incline. He really hoped that they were closing in on Tyler and his dad.

"Guess we better go see what's on the other side," Justin said as he got to his feet, his clothes still dripping onto the ground. "Max, you are hard-core, pal."

Justin and Carmen walked their bikes, and the group began trudging up the hill. Huffing and puffing, they arrived at the top of a ridge. The sun was high above them now. Their clothes had already dried in the heat.

Directly beneath them, a steep and rocky mountain dropped off sharply into a ravine about a hundred feet across. They stood for a moment looking around at the expansive view and catching their breath.

Justin scanned the horizon. About a mile in the distance, he saw a strip of highway. Tiny cars zipped across it like toys on a plastic racetrack. He looked a little closer. About halfway down the mountain and to the right, an old wooden railroad bridge extended across the ravine. Even from his vantage point, he could see that the bridge was in bad shape. There were gaping holes in the bottom and planks dangling off the sides. Just beyond it was the churning stream they had crossed and the waterfall.

Max leaned over the edge and looked down the mountain. He started to growl. Justin followed his gaze and saw a campground in a large clearing tucked behind a stand of trees. Tyler, Stack, and Emilio sat on rocks around the edge. They weren't talking. They looked like they were just . . . waiting.

Justin scanned the campground, until his eyes fell on the sight he had been hoping for. His heart leaped in his chest. Tyler's truck was parked at the back of the clearing with the passenger side window down. Justin could just make out a familiar figure in the cab.

It was his dad—he was alive.

"Look," Justin whispered to his friends, "now that we know my dad's okay, I think someone should go for help. Those psychos buying Tyler's guns could be here any second. But I'm not leaving my dad here by himself."

Carmen nodded, her face serious. "I'll head for that road." She pointed at the highway in the distance. "And I'll come back with the police."

"How about some Navy Seals?" Chuy said, only half joking. "Why don't we just use my cell phone?" he asked, pulling it out of his pocket.

"They won't be able to track us closely enough," Justin said. "They'll just ping the closest tower, and then it could take a while for them to find this spot. It'll be faster if you go get someone."

"How do you know all that?" Carmen asked.

Justin shrugged. His cheeks felt hot.

He had been so grateful that Carmen and Chuy wanted to help him, but now he just wanted to get them as far away from this scene as possible.

"Go with her, Chuy," Justin said. "I got this."

"No way, J. I'm not leaving you alone out here."

"I'll be fine," Carmen insisted.

Justin could tell from the looks on their faces that they weren't going to take no for an answer. He forced himself not to worry that Carmen was going to be alone. Even in the short time he'd known her, he'd already figured out that she could take care of herself. He looked at her, and they held each other's gaze. Justin's whole body felt strange—like he was floating, but also kind of like someone was squeezing the air out of his lungs. Sort of like when he had jumped across Cutter's Doom.

"You need to go," Justin managed to squeak out.

"Yeah," she said. "But before I do—" She stepped forward and planted her lips on his. Justin was so startled that he didn't know what to do at first. Then he quickly came to his senses and kissed her back.

"I am *not* seeing this," Chuy muttered.

Carmen pulled away from Justin, hopped on her bike, and disappeared into the trees—all before Justin could take a breath.

Justin stood still, reliving the kiss for a moment. His thoughts were interrupted by the loud ring of a cell phone. Justin spun around to see Chuy staring in horror at the phone in his hand.

"Answer it!" Justin said in an angry whisper.

Chuy fumbled with the phone, so nervous that he couldn't get his fingers on the right buttons. The phone jingled again. Chuy finally managed to pick it up midring.

"Hola," Chuy whispered into the phone.

Justin could hear Chuy's mom speaking frantically in Spanish. As Chuy tried to calm her down and get off the phone as fast as possible, Justin leaned over the edge and looked at the guys down below. They must have heard Chuy's phone ring. They were on their feet, guns in hand, scanning the trees. Stack's evil Rottweiler, the one who had survived Max's attack, was crouched down low, growling and sniffing at the air.

Justin snatched the phone from Chuy's hand and hit the End button. But it was too late. The men below knew they were there.

TWENTY-ONE

EVERYTHING TURNED INTO TOTAL CHAOS.

Justin watched as the Rottweiler caught their scent and barked frantically up in their direction. Stack spun around in circles, waving a gun in the air. Emilio ran around the truck and grabbed a shotgun. Justin's dad peered through the windshield of the truck, looking for some sign of what was happening.

Only Tyler was calm, which made sense—he was a trained soldier. He stood at the center of the clearing, slowly scanning the forest.

"Get 'em, Draco!" Tyler commanded the dog. The Rottweiler shot out of the clearing, straight up the hill.

His muscles flexed and pumped as he powered his massive bulk through the underbrush. He looked like a tank, barreling right for Justin, Chuy, and Max—a tank with a really scary look in his eyes.

Justin took a deep breath, trying to slow down his heart rate. He needed to stay level-headed. He crouched down next to Max, who stood at the edge of the drop-off, growling. Max's body was tensed up, and his ears were flattened against his head. He was preparing for battle.

"You ready for round two?" Justin whispered to him. Max let out a little snarl in response.

Just at that moment, the Rottweiler leaped over the top of the ridge and froze, his legs splayed out in a fighting stance, growling deeply at Max.

"Dude," Chuy said, "that is one scary mutt."

All the fur on Max's back stood on end. The dogs circled each other slowly, never taking their eyes off each other.

"Max . . ." Justin began. He hated to see his dog fight, but he knew there was no way around it. Max was trained for this—he could *win* this battle. And Max was their only hope of escaping the aggressive beast that could kill Justin or Chuy with one bite to the neck.

Suddenly, Draco sprang forward, lunging at Max, slamming into him with all his might. Max let out a loud yelp and fell sideways onto the ground. The Rottweiler landed on top of him with a sickening *thud*, and the two dogs rolled around in a ferocious blur of fur and bared teeth. The harsh sound of their snarls and the horrifying snaps of powerful jaws filled the air. Max and the Rottweiler were locked in a particularly gruesome hold, their fangs digging into each other's necks.

"No!" Justin cried. Chuy just gasped. Max was taking the worst of it.

Desperate to help his dog, Justin lifted his bike over his head and swung it at the Rottweiler. He whacked him, hard, across the back, knocking him off Max. Draco somersaulted a few feet away, regained his balance, and ran toward Justin, his fangs bared. Justin froze. Out of the corner of his eye, he saw Max righting himself and moving into position.

"Max," Justin said, slowly stepping backward without taking his eyes off the Rottweiler, "he's bigger and stronger than you are, so you need to fight smart, okay?"

It was as if Max understood Justin's words. He

took off like a shot, zipping around Justin, past the Rottweiler, and flying over the edge of the cliff. His body arced gracefully into the air for a split second, and then he was gone.

Draco tore his evil gaze from Justin and flew after Max, disappearing down the steep mountain. Justin and Chuy could hear the dogs as they tumbled and fought all the way down. Justin stepped to the edge and watched as Max reached the bottom first, and took off into the clearing. The Rottweiler, dazed but still fierce, scrambled to his feet and raced after Max. Max was a smarter dog, no question—and his slim frame meant that he had more stamina, even if he wasn't as strong. He slowed down and let Draco almost catch up to him, then just as the distance between them closed up, Max sped up again. He led the Rottweiler around the clearing, through the trees, and toward the bridge and the waterfall beyond it.

Justin knew how amazing Max was, but even he couldn't believe what he was seeing. *Max was trying to exhaust the bigger dog. He was fighting with his brain.*

"Attaboy," Justin whispered to himself.

Justin's mind raced. He didn't even have time to consider the fact that he had nearly gotten killed by a pumped-up Rottweiler. He was too worried about Max, scared for his dad, and desperately trying to figure out a way out of this.

Just then, Justin and Chuy heard the sound of footsteps—and Tyler and Emilio's angry voices. They were getting closer.

Chuy's face wore an expression of sheer terror.

"It's okay, man," Justin reassured his friend. "But we need to split up," he instructed.

Chuy nodded. He took a deep breath and seemed to find his last drop of hidden courage. "Okay, J.," Chuy said, his voice steady. "Meet you back here in a minute. Cool?"

"Cool," Justin replied, hopping on his bike. "Let's go."

Tyler and Emilio burst through the trees.

"What's up, cuz?" Chuy taunted Emilio before bolting into the woods on foot.

"Get back here you little—" Emilio screamed, taking after Chuy.

Tyler eyed Justin menacingly. Before Tyler could speak, Justin hit the pedals on his bike and flew straight past him, nearly knocking Tyler over as he whizzed by. He sped down a path that led into the woods and sloped sharply downward. To his left, the narrow road dropped off sharply. Gripping his handlebars, Justin steered over the tree stumps and rocky terrain. He heard twigs snapping under his tires, and Tyler swearing behind him.

After a few minutes, Justin heard voices ahead of him on the path. He slowed down and listened carefully. It was Chuy and Emilio. Justin came around a bend and saw Emilio's back turned toward him. Emilio's arm was raised, and Justin's heart plummeted. Emilio was pointing a gun right at Chuy, who held his hands up in the air. Chuy saw Justin, but kept his expression neutral so Emilio wouldn't know Justin was behind him. Justin nodded to Chuy to let his friend know that he had a plan to help him.

"It didn't have to go down like this," Emilio spat. Chuy just shrugged, trying not to raise suspicion.

Justin rode up slowly and quietly behind Emilio. Just as Emilio pulled back the safety on his gun, Justin picked up speed and raised his front tire in a perfect wheelie. Emilio turned, but not fast enough to get out of the way. Justin slammed into him, full force, his tire smacking Emilio right in the chest and knocking him off his feet. Emilio's gun fired into the sky, and then he flew backward, over the side of the path. He disappeared from view, but Chuy and Justin could hear him grunting and swearing as he rolled and bounced down the hill toward the clearing at the bottom, bashing into roots and rocks as he went.

"Nice one, J.," Chuy exclaimed.

"Thanks. You okay?" Justin asked.

Chuy looked down at his body, making a show of examining himself. "Looks like it," he said with a grin. "Now stop chitchatting, and let's go get your dad."

Justin and Chuy took off down the path, Justin riding and Chuy running at his side. They followed the dirt road as it angled steeply downhill and spiraled inward. They finally emerged at the edge of the clearing. The railroad bridge and river were behind them.

Emilio rolled back and forth on the ground a few yards away, clutching his right leg and writhing in pain.

"My leg!" Emilio shouted. "It's broken!"

"Stay with him," Justin shouted to Chuy. "Make sure he doesn't cause any more trouble." Chuy nodded and stood near—but not too near—his wailing cousin.

Justin didn't care about Emilio or his broken leg—he only wanted to find his father. He spotted Ray all the way across the wide clearing, near Tyler's truck. Justin froze. He couldn't believe what he was seeing. To his horror, he saw Max running at his dad, and his dad pointing a gun straight at Justin's dog.

TWENTY-TWO

JUSTIN ABSORBED THE SCENE ALL AT ONCE: MAX CHARGing at his dad, with his teeth bared and his ears low and pointed backward. Justin's dad pointing the gun right at Max, a confused look on his face. *He thought Max was going to attack him.*

What his dad couldn't see—which Justin and Max both could see—was that Stack was running at Justin's dad from behind, holding a giant rock in his fleshy hands, raised high in the air. He was about to slam it down onto Justin's dad's head.

Justin was too far away to help. He'd never make it the hundred yards or so across the clearing in time. He sucked in his breath as Max hurtled himself forward.

Mercifully, his dad didn't shoot. Instead, he ducked and lowered the gun. Just as he did, Stack brought the rock down but missed. Stack stumbled, and Max flew over Ray and crashed into Stack's chest, knocking him to the ground. Max stood on top of the giant deputy, snarling just inches from his face, but there was no need for such vigilance: Stack was out cold.

"Dad!" Justin called out as he rode quickly over to his father. Ray's head shot up at the sound of his son's voice, and a look of pure relief washed over his face. Justin felt his chest swell with gratitude that his dad was okay, but he still felt bad that he'd gotten them both into this situation in the first place. "Are you okay?" Justin asked.

"I'm fine," he said as Justin skidded to a stop next to him. His dad stumbled forward, wrapping Justin in a tight hug and letting out a choked cry of relief. Justin almost couldn't believe it—he and his dad never hugged. But he certainly wasn't complaining. In fact, he was surprised at how much he liked it. "Max here saved me," his dad went on, pulling away and looking Justin over from head to toe. "Are you okay?" Justin nodded. His dad searched the clearing behind Justin. "You bring anyone else with you?"

"Besides Max?" Justin shook his head. "Just Carmen and Chuy."

His dad reached out and punched him lightly on the shoulder. "And I thought you were supposed to be the smart one in the family," he said with a grin. Justin couldn't help but chuckle. He was right—they weren't exactly the cavalry.

"Tyler's on my tail, Dad. He's going to be back here any second," Justin said.

His dad thought for a moment, weighing their options. "We should head for the highway, as fast as we can," he said.

Justin eyed Tyler's truck nearby. "Why not take that?" he asked.

"Because Tyler has the keys. But that doesn't mean he'll be able to drive it." With that, Justin's dad raised the gun in his hand and aimed it at the truck.

"Dad—there's a whole load of weapons in there!" Justin cried.

"Don't worry, son—they're all in the back." His dad fired one shot into the front right tire and two into the grill, piercing the radiator with a hiss. "That ought to slow him down."

Justin was impressed. He'd never seen his dad act

like . . . well, like a Marine in combat before. Justin, his dad, and Max headed out of the clearing and into the woods. Justin pushed his bike and his dad limped alongside him. They moved as quickly as they could, but together their progress over the rough terrain was pretty slow.

They hadn't made it that far when Justin's dad stopped and turned to his son. "This is crazy," he said. "I'm just slowing you down."

As he spoke, they heard the sound of a rattling, wheezing, but definitely still functioning truck engine heading right for them.

"So much for shooting out the radiator," Justin's dad said grimly. "Listen, son, you and Max head for the highway. I'll keep these idiots off of you."

Justin felt a surge of mixed emotions. He wanted so badly to let his dad know how sorry he was for everything—and how relieved he was that he was safe. There was no time for that, though—the sound of the engine grew louder.

Justin thought hard. There was a way out of this—he just had to figure out what it was. An idea came to him that was shaky at best, but he knew he had no choice but to try it. He shook his head. "No way, Dad," he said firmly. "Every time I'm in trouble, Max takes the fight away from me to keep me safe." Max must have heard his name, because he nudged his head into Justin's hand. Justin felt Max's soft fur under his palm. "What kind of a person would I be if I didn't do the same thing for my own dad?"

Without waiting for a response, Justin hopped on his bike and sped back in the direction they had come—straight for the truck. Max galloped along at his side.

"Justin!" his dad screamed. "*Justin*—you need to listen to me—head for the highway . . ."

He couldn't hear his dad anymore over the roar of the busted engine. Suddenly, the truck appeared on the path in front of him, steam spewing from the front hood, one tire flat as a pancake and flopping instead of turning. Stack was driving, an outraged look on his face. Tyler sat in the passenger seat, his expression cold but furious. It sent a chill down Justin's spine.

Justin waited until Tyler's eyes locked on his, then he veered off onto a narrow dirt road that cut through the trees and banked uphill at a sharp angle. The truck couldn't follow him. He looked back over his shoulder to see Stack slam on the brakes and Tyler hop out of the car. The plan was unfolding exactly as Justin had hoped it would.

Perfect. Tyler was going to follow him on foot. Justin could definitely outrace him on his bike.

Justin pumped his legs hard to steer the bike up to the ridge. He heard Max running nearby, and Tyler huffing and puffing at a distance behind them. Together, Justin and Max zigzagged uphill until they reached the top. They rode on flat land for a moment, then the ground sloped downward again. They headed down as fast as they could, Tyler gaining some ground behind them.

Justin pedaled faster and let gravity speed him up. He lifted his front tire over the bigger rocks and roots, then dropped back down onto both wheels again. He had no idea where they were headed, but he knew he didn't want to give Tyler the chance to catch up to them.

The ground leveled off, and then he saw it, just a few hundred yards straight ahead: the ravine, which was as deep and wide as Cutter's Doom.

Justin and Max were hurtling toward the gaping chasm at top speed, and there was no time to stop.

It was also his best shot at losing Tyler for good.

Justin pedaled harder.

"Come on, Max—you can do this!" he called out

as he approached the cliff's edge. At precisely the right second, Justin lifted his front tire and sailed up and out, and Max leaped forward next to him. They hurtled through the air. Justin felt gravity release him for just a moment, and the air whipped through his hair and across his face. He clutched his handlebars tightly, his stomach swooping and blood pounding in his ears.

He and Max were flying, side by side.

Then, with an abrupt jerk, Justin's front tire landed hard on the ground on the other side of the ravine. He had made it across—but barely. His back tire slipped over the edge of the cliff, and the weight of his bike pulled him backward. Justin let go of the handlebars and threw himself onto solid ground. He cleared the bike just as it disappeared down the hill. It had served him well, but Chuy's brother wasn't going to be happy that his bike was now at the bottom of a ditch.

Justin hopped to his feet and looked around, expecting Max to run up beside him. But he didn't. Justin's heart stopped as he looked back and saw Max dangling off the edge of the drop-off, his front paws stretched way out in front of him, sliding in the dirt. He struggled to pull himself up, his back legs clambering and scratching at the face of the cliff. Loose pebbles flew all around him and pinged off the side of the hill on their way down.

Justin raced over to him, but he wasn't fast enough.

Max's claws couldn't catch hold.

Justin registered the fear in his dog's eyes and he heard Max's desperate yelping as the dog slipped backward and out of sight, down the steep slope and toward the ground below.

"MAX!" Justin screamed. Reaching the edge, Justin looked down and watched, horrified, as Max tumbled down the steep hill. Halfway down he slammed into a narrow ledge and came to a stop. Justin exhaled a huge sigh of relief when Max rolled over, got to his feet, and shook himself off, sending a cloud of dust into the air. Max looked up at Justin and barked a few times to let him know he was okay. Then Max moved in a tight circle, trying to figure out how to get down from his perch.

Justin frantically tried to find a way to help Max. He couldn't climb down to him—he'd never be able to help Max get up or down, and they both might end up stuck. Max sniffed at the side of the cliff and scratched at the dirt.

"It's okay, Max," Justin called down to him. "You're okay, pal." Before Justin could figure out what to do, he heard a sound behind him and spun around, his heart pounding in his chest.

Tyler was coming straight for him.

TWENTY-THREE

JUSTIN TOOK OFF, TYLER FAST ON HIS HEELS. JUSTIN headed straight into the woods, hoping the trees would provide some cover. As he ran, he searched desperately for an escape route. Suddenly, he spotted the old, crumbling railroad bridge, jutting out from the hillside off to his right and crossing the river.

It was his best shot.

Justin sprinted toward the bridge, which got bigger as he got closer, until finally it loomed over him. He stopped to catch his breath and studied the ancient-looking structure—or what was left of it anyway. It had clearly been out of use for a long time. There were entire sections missing, either rotted away or broken by years of use, then abandonment. It was suspended probably fifty feet above the ground, and stretched at least a hundred feet across. The river flowed beneath it.

Tyler's footsteps crashed through the bushes behind him. *He was closing in.*

Justin had no choice. He put one foot onto the first plank of wood, and the whole bridge dipped and swayed. He swallowed hard, then took another shaky step. The wood beneath him shuddered. He gripped the splintering railing and looked down. Bad idea, he quickly realized. Better not to see how far there was to fall.

Where was Max? Justin hoped he'd gotten down from the ledge, but he didn't see him anywhere below or in the woods around him.

Justin took another shaky step, his eyes locked firmly on the long, treacherous path before him. He had to avoid the holes and pieces of board that were clearly not strong enough to support him.

Suddenly, the entire bridge lurched and wobbled. Justin looked over his shoulder and saw Tyler racing toward him, clutching a handgun. Tyler didn't seem to care that the bridge was about to fall apart. He had a fierce and frightening look in his eyes. It was pretty clear Tyler cared about only one thing: getting his hands on Justin.

"There's no way out of this, Justin," Tyler shouted after him. "You may as well give up now."

"No way," Justin yelled back, without turning around. He tried to pick up the pace, but was worried the whole bridge was about to collapse under their weight.

Justin heard a sputtering engine in the distance, quickly growing louder. He looked down through the bridge to see Tyler's truck driving through the ravine below them, still spewing smoke.

"My backup is here, kid," Tyler called. "You're on your own out here."

Before Justin had a chance to respond to Tyler's taunts, he saw a figure dart out in front of the vehicle. The man waved his arms at the car. Justin gasped: It was his dad, who pointed a gun straight at the windshield and fired.

The truck swerved and crashed into the side of the hill. The back of the truck exploded in a burst of flame, and suddenly a thousand gunshots pinged around the ravine. The ammunition in Tyler's truck had ignited.

Tyler and Justin both dropped to their stomachs, covering their heads with their arms and lying flat against the boards. Bullets thwacked into the bridge all around them.

After the explosion, everything went silent. His eardrums hummed. Justin peered down through a wide hole in the bridge. His heart nearly burst with relief and happiness when he saw his dad crouched behind a huge rock. *He was okay.* Justin just hoped that Max wasn't anywhere near the blast.

When the smoke started to settle, Tyler scrambled to his feet and continued his advance on Justin.

"You can't get away from me, you little—" Tyler slipped on a shard of wood, which snapped off and fell to the ground, landing with a distant crunch. He got up, wobbling and tipping as the bridge moved, but he kept coming.

"The cops are on their way," Justin yelled. "You're never going to get away with this!"

"Cops? How are they going to find you out in the middle of nowhere?" Tyler replied, moving a few steps closer to Justin. "Besides, I don't think the sheriff is going to care very much," he finished with a nasty laugh.

Suddenly, a second loud explosion rocked the canyon and sent a spray of fire and light shooting into the air. A hot blast of air knocked Justin off his feet. The fire had made its way around to the back of Tyler's truck, setting off the rocket launchers in the cargo hold. Justin and Tyler ducked for cover, putting their hands over their heads.

Tyler got up again and lurched forward, waving his gun in the air.

"I'll kill you before I let you get out of here," Tyler snarled.

Justin forced himself to his feet, ready to run. He took a step, then stopped short: The rocket launcher had blown a gaping hole in the bridge, right in front of him. He swung his arms in the air, desperate for balance, catching himself just before he tipped forward and fell the fifty feet to the ground.

He spun around to face Tyler, who was closing in on him.

There was nowhere for Justin to go.

Justin froze, considering his options. He could stay where he was and hope Tyler fell through the crumbling bridge before he reached him. Or he could face Tyler like Kyle would have—like a hero.

Justin spun around just as Tyler was closing in on him. He could see the sweat pouring off Tyler's face, a look of pure hatred in his bloodshot eyes. He leveled the gun at Justin.

Justin's vision narrowed to the pinpoint of the gun barrel, which was aimed right at his chest. His body vibrated with fear, but he couldn't let that stop him. He reached down and snatched up a large, splintery plank of wood and held it up like a bat. He would go down fighting.

"Tyler!" Justin's dad called out from below. "Don't you dare hurt my boy!"

Tyler ignored him and pressed forward until he stood just inches from Justin. He leaned in, his breath hot on Justin's face.

"It didn't have to end like this, kid," Tyler said, his voice cold. "But Kyle always said you were gonna surprise everyone one day." Justin's heart pounded in his chest. "I just don't think this is what he had in mind," Tyler finished quietly, his eyes digging into Justin's.

They stared at each other. Out of the corner of his eye, Justin saw a flash of movement behind Tyler. Relief flooded him. It was Max—he had somehow gotten down off the side of the cliff and found Justin. Now he was in full aggressive war dog mode, heading straight for Tyler's back.

"What do you think Kyle would say about this situation?" Tyler asked, glowering at Justin.

Justin smiled at Tyler. Tyler shot him a confused look.

"I think he'd say," Justin began, "Max, *attack*!"

Tyler's eyes went big and round as he registered what was happening. He spun around and tried to steady his gun, but he was too late to help himself. Justin kicked out Tyler's leg and Tyler fell to his knees, firing a shot into the air. With a giant roar, Max leaped onto Tyler's chest and locked his mighty jaw around Tyler's shoulder. Justin sprang out of the way as Tyler went flying backward, but Max didn't let go. Instead, Max just clamped down harder on Tyler's arm, pressing himself against Tyler's body as together they fell through the giant hole in the bridge. The two plunged downward, spiraling as they fell. Max didn't let go of Tyler, loyal until the very end.

"Max!" Justin screamed. He dropped to his stomach and looked down through the hole. Sirens screamed in the distance, getting louder and closer as Justin tried to absorb what he saw.

Tyler lay across a giant rock at a painfully awkward angle, his body bent and twisted. On top of him lay Max. Justin's dog wasn't moving.

TWENTY-FOUR

JUSTIN LIKED IT HERE IN THE CEMETERY. IT WAS QUIET and peaceful, and he felt as if it was the first time he'd been able to think straight in weeks. He tugged at a few loose blades of dry grass, then tossed them aside.

The afternoon sun warmed his face, but the heat wasn't so oppressive anymore. Summer was winding down, and he could feel the first hint of fall in the air. That meant school would be starting soon. For the first time ever, that didn't sound so awful to him. After all, Carmen was transferring to his school.

Justin's hand absentmindedly found Max's head and scratched between his ears. Max nuzzled Justin's fingers and let out a little *mwaaamp* noise—that cross between a yawn, a snort, and a whimper. It was the dog sound for contentment and affection that Justin loved to hear. Max dropped his head onto his front paws and thumped his tail into the grass a few times.

Justin patted Max's side, careful to avoid the stitches and bandages that would be there for another week or two at least. Max was pretty banged up, but he'd come out remarkably well, considering the battle he'd had with the devil dog and the fifty-foot drop he'd survived.

Justin ran his hand through Max's soft fur and stared at his brother's gravestone.

"Hey, Kyle," he began, faltering at first. He'd never sat in a cemetery before, let alone talked to one of its residents. He paused, then decided he had nothing to lose—and plenty to say.

"People always said you were a great Marine," Justin started again. "And you were. I'll never be like you, and maybe I figured out that I don't want to be. And that's okay." Justin paused. A plane flew overhead, and a gas lawn mower chugged along somewhere in the distance. Max rolled onto his side and stretched out next to Justin, his ears twitching as a slight breeze picked up and new sounds floated in their direction.

"I know we didn't always get along too well," Justin said softly to his brother's headstone, "and I was really mad when you left for the Marines. But I guess lots of brothers are like that sometimes. I'm just sorry we'll never get the chance to grow up together and be friends." Justin's throat felt tight, and hot tears pooled up in his eyes.

"I just want to thank you for Max. And tell you I love you. As long as I live, Kyle, I'll never forget you."

An image flashed through Justin's mind: It was Kyle's face the day he told Justin and their parents that he was going to work with a military dog. Justin had long forgotten about that conversation, but he replayed it now as if it had happened yesterday. Kyle was so excited talking about the incredible dogs that fought alongside soldiers all over the world—he was practically beaming, and he said he couldn't wait to meet his new partner. "The dogs are like family to their handlers," Kyle had said.

Justin got to his feet. Max hopped up with him. They stood together, side by side, looking at Kyle's grave. Justin read his brother's name for the hundredth time, and the words MARINE, SON, BROTHER, HERO.

Justin raised his hand to his brow, offering his brother a quick salute, just like Kyle had taught him to do. Then he turned and hopped on his bike. Justin rode off for home, Max trotting along at his side.

TWENTY-FIVE

JUSTIN LEANED HIS BIKE AGAINST THE SIDE OF THE house and headed into the backyard. He stopped short when he saw what was there—or, more accurately, what wasn't there. Max's cage was gone.

Justin grinned and opened the back door. He stepped into the kitchen and breathed in the scent of his mother's pot roast. It was the best smell on earth. Max sauntered in behind him and let out a happy yap. His tail wagged so hard he whacked Justin's mom with it a couple of times. She chuckled and gave Max a scratch on the back of the neck. Max wiggled over to Carmen and Chuy, who both dropped to their knees and wrapped their arms around him.

Max sniffed at the air. His tail wagged even harder.

"Yeah, Max," Carmen said, letting him lick her nose, "we've got some carnitas cooking for you tonight."

Pamela closed the stove and tossed an oven mitt onto the counter. She took two big steps over to Justin and wrapped her arms around him, squeezing him in a hug so tight it forced the breath out of him.

"Mom," he managed to squeak out, "are you going to do this every time I come home now?"

His mom didn't release her grip.

"Yup," she said. "Every time you're an hour late coming home from a walk, you bet your behind I will." She let him go, and he took a couple of quick breaths. "Where on earth have you been anyway?"

"Out cleaning up Gotham," Chuy said from across the room. "Taking out villains, right, buddy?"

"Well," Carmen said with a silly grin, "you know he needs to be a superhero if he's going to be my *boyfriend*."

Justin laughed, blushing a little at the word that was still so new to him. But there was no denying it—he *liked* the word, especially when Carmen was saying it.

But there was still something Justin needed to get off his chest. His expression turned serious. He turned to Chuy. He hadn't been sure how to phrase what he needed to tell his friend, but he was starting to figure out that it was more important to say something than to say it perfectly.

"Chuy, man, I'm glad you're here," Justin began. "And I'm really sorry—I know your family must be upset about Emilio going to—"

Chuy cut him off. "Emilio belongs in jail, man. You did the right thing, and we all know that. That dude was bad news for my family, too."

Justin was so relieved to hear that Chuy felt that way. He and Chuy shook hands.

Justin's dad appeared in the doorway from the living room, still in his work uniform. Max ran over to him and sniffed at his legs. Ray patted Max lightly on the top of the head.

"Well, hello, everyone," he said with a wave.

"Hey, Mr. Wincott," Chuy and Carmen said at once.

"Hi, honey," Justin's mom said.

"Hey, Dad," Justin said. "Where's Max's cage?"

His dad shrugged and said, "At the junkyard, on top of the pile. Where it belongs. He'll be staying in the house with us from now on. Where *he* belongs."

Justin and his dad held each other's gaze, both of them unsure where to go from here. They'd been through a lot together this summer, and now they were in new territory.

"What do you say to your father?" Justin's mom asked.

"It's about time," Justin said with a straight face. There was a beat of awkward silence, then everyone burst out laughing.

"That's cold!" Chuy said, pretend-punching Justin on the shoulder. Max immediately began barking and raced over to Justin's side. He positioned himself between Chuy and Justin, his ears back.

"It's okay, Max!" Justin laughed. "He's our friend. Take it easy." Max sniffed at Chuy and wagged his tail again. Chuy let out an exaggerated sigh of relief.

Everyone started chatting again—Pamela, Chuy, and Carmen picked up their conversation about the merits of various dog breeds, while Pamela stirred a giant pot on the stovetop.

Justin watched his friend, his girlfriend, and his mom together and felt an ache in his chest he'd never felt before. It was a new, funny combination of happiness, contentment, love, gratitude—and a big, healthy dose of sadness that his brother wasn't here to share all this with him and their parents.

Justin felt his father's eyes on him. He looked up to where he still stood in the doorway. Justin wondered if his dad was thinking the same things he was. They exchanged a long look, and Justin gave his dad a half smile. Ray didn't quite smile back, but he nodded at Justin, and Justin saw something in his dad's expression that he'd never seen there before: respect.

Max gently pressed his nose into Justin's palm. Justin looked down at him.

"You hungry, buddy?" he asked, squatting down so he and Max were eye to eye. Max pressed his snout against Justin's cheek and snuffled in his ear.

Justin stroked Max's head.

"That's my boy, Max," he said. "That's my boy."

NOTE

Dogs have been used in the U.S. military
since World War I.

More than 3,000 dogs have served in
Iraq and Afghanistan since 1993.

More than 60 dogs and 40 of their handlers have been
killed in the service of their country in those wars.

This story is dedicated to their memory.